When The Eagle Cried

Vicki Cook

ISBN: 0692507485
ISBN 13: 9780692507483

Dedication

For my mother and father, Christine and Leon; I love that I grew up in the country sunshine and running the woods from daylight until dark. I would not trade my childhood for anything. There are so many things that I am grateful to you both for, but my dedication would be longer than my book if I were to list them all. I want to say thank you for everything. With all my love, forever!

And special thanks to Shoshanna for your help and encouragement.

Books by:

Vicki Cook

Wilderness Princess

Morgan's Journey

Heavenly Father,

Cover me with Your grace so that I could live each day in a way that would give You glory.

By Your grace for Your glory!

Amen

Table of Contents

Chapter 1

MICAH TREMBLED WITH excitement as she pulled the wedding dress into place. She had been waiting three years for this day. That was when she and her family moved to the area and Micah first met the Phillips family. There was the father, mother, three sons and a daughter. Jewel Phillips and Micah had become like sisters, but one of Jewel's brothers had caught Micah's eye. Robert, he was the source of Micah being in a whirlwind of emotions and excitement today.

Jewel entered the room and laughed when she saw the flustered bride. "Here, let me help," she offered. Jewel had helped with the sewing of the wedding dress and with the details of the wedding. She would also be standing as Micah's maid of honor today. The two girls had spent many hours fussing with the cabin over on Mill's Creek in preparation for the newlyweds, while Robert and his brother had been in charge of all outside repairs. The cabin was sound and in good shape even though it had been abandoned a few years back.

Robert's father had passed away last year, leaving the care of their mother to rest on the shoulders of the children. This care was mostly symbolic. She was quite capable of caring for herself. Robert was the oldest of four children, followed by Taylor, then Jewel, and finally, Paul.

Micah was the youngest of three children. Abby, the oldest, was married before they moved westward three years ago. She had remained behind in Boston with her husband and his family. Ben, the middle child, had married a year after they had settled here. He was the proud father of an infant son. He and his family lived about eight miles west of the family farm.

Robert was twenty-one and Micah had recently turned eighteen. She had wanted to wed sooner, but her father had said she must wait until after her eighteenth birthday and Robert had agreed that waiting would be best. Micah had figured the main reason for her father's wishes was the fact Micah's mother had passed away and both of her siblings had already left home with only Micah remaining. He most likely wanted to hang on to her as long as possible; after all, she was his baby girl.

Papa's baby girl was how he had referred to her for as long as she could remember and she treasured the special name in her heart. She had been torn between her desire to be with Robert and part of her still wishing to cling to her father. She had not fussed much about her father's decision.

The wedding had gone as Micah had pictured it in her imagination. It was not fancy, just special. She had been smitten with Robert the moment she laid eyes on him and that had grown into love and continued to grow with each passing day. Micah had wondered if Robert felt any wedding jitters like her. Her curiosity was satisfied when he began to stammer when repeating his vows.

Robert and Micah were settling into their new routine as husband and wife. Micah was still in a dream world with married life. Cooking, cleaning, and laundry were a joy. She was not sure Robert felt so smitten with his role as husband. He seemed to continually worry about his responsibilities.

The wedding had taken place soon after the first of the year. Robert and Micah had been advised to marry then by several couples in the community. They had reasoned that doing so at this time of year would allow them time to be together and get to know each other, whereas if they waited until spring most of their time would be spent planting and preparing for the coming winter. Family and community would pitch in to supply them with foods to hold them through the first few months. Micah thought this sounded like valid reasoning, but for her it mostly meant she would be marrying Robert five months sooner. She had been waiting for three years to marry him and any time she could shave off the waiting period would be eagerly eliminated.

Micah began noticing little signs of her wedding bliss coming to a halt. Robert seemed to be getting edgy with her and the closer spring planting came, the more distant and restless he had become. He was even short tempered at times. When she would question him as to the reason he would reply that nothing was wrong. Then Robert began spending more and more time away from the cabin. Micah's heart began to break. She had thought that she and Robert would have a marriage where when a problem presented itself it would be discussed and dealt with. Instead, she found herself on the outside of something major. He was apparently turning to others with his problems. One thing certain, he was not turning to her for comfort. The thought haunted her and was constantly running through the back of her mind. Maybe, just maybe, he had been rethinking his marriage to her and thought it a mistake. Maybe distancing himself was the only way he knew how to deal with the mistake. Micah had seen this tactic used in marriages where the couple survived by avoiding each other. The thought of such a wretched marriage had always taken Micah's breath. Now here she stood just months after her fairy tale wedding facing the very thing she despised. More sinister thoughts began to follow. What if Robert had taken notice of one of the other girls? Micah had not been the only one to think he was quite a catch and he would not be the first person in a similar situation to look elsewhere. She was positive Robert was not that type of person when she married him, but now nothing made sense. She had never dreamed anything like this would be happening, either. Micah could feel uncertainty slipping its way into her heart. Her love for Robert was as it always had been, but for the first time she began to question Robert's love for her.

Micah was drying the lunch dishes and putting them away when she heard Robert say her name.

"Micah?"

"What?" she asked, absently as she turned to face him.

"What's wrong?"

"Nothing," she said, shaking her head and raising her eyebrows in a questioning gesture.

"Then why have you been so quiet lately?" he asked.

Micah shrugged and turned away, trying to dismiss the matter, but Robert was determined to get an answer.

"Micah," he gently pursued, "it's not like you to be so quiet and distant..."

"Distant!" she countered. "I've been distant!" she whirled around to face him. "You have hardly had two words to say to me for nearly a month and when

I ask what's wrong you push me even farther away. What is it for you, Robert? Have you suddenly decided I was a mistake? And maybe you should have picked one of the other girls! And the nerve of you saying I'm quirky when you are the biggest quirk in this house right now!" She finished as a hot tears streamed down her flushed face.

Robert stared at Micah, momentarily taken aback by her outburst.

"What?" Robert finally managed, "what are you talking about?"

Micah stood hands on hips, waiting for answers to the questions racing through her mind.

"Micah," he began, "we need to talk…"

Micah gave a "humph!" sound that was loaded with 'do you think?' attitude.

Just then a knock sounded at the door. Robert turned and reached for the door as Micah wiped her tears on the dishtowel. Robert opened the door to find his brother, Paul.

"Robert, you have to come quick," he said excitedly, "one of the cows strayed into the marsh and now she's bogged down in the mud," he finished as he gasped for air.

"Go on ahead, I'll be along," Robert promised.

"You have to hurry. Taylor is with her now, but she's been there quite a while. Taylor said she can't take much more strugglin'," Paul urged.

"All right, I'm coming," disgust crept into his voice as he closed the door. Robert turned and crossed the room to where Micah still stood with her back to the door and placed his hands on her shoulders.

"I'll be back as soon as I can, then we *will* talk," he assured her, "until then, stop crying," and with that he left.

So there was a problem. Had she been right? It was Robert's last statement that stuck in her mind and began to trouble her the most. "Until then, stop crying" was he expecting her to cry more? Micah was miserable not knowing the truth.

It was well after dark and Micah was still in misery waiting for Robert to return. Her heart quickened when she heard his horse call to the one still in the barn stall. Robert had missed supper and she found it impossible to eat. She had pushed the kettle of stew to the back of the stove. Micah added wood to the stove and pulled the kettle to the front to warm.

When Robert came into the house, he was covered in mud from head to toe. One glance told her he was exhausted. Micah wanted answers now, but made herself wait.

"Did you get her out?" she asked as she handed him clean dry clothes.

"Yea, but not the way we wanted. We tried to pull her free of the mud, but she just wouldn't budge. We nearly strangled her trying, finally," he hesitated, "we shot her."

Micah gasped, "Shot her?"

Robert nodded, "yea, Paul and Taylor took her home with them. She's only good for eating now."

Micah blinked away the tears threatening to fall. She knew sometimes things had to be, but it still made her sad when those times would come about.

"I'm sorry about your cow," she said softly.

"Our cow," Robert corrected her with a smile as he buttoned up his clean shirt, "that brings us to another matter that needs to be taken care of right quick." Robert put his arms around Micah and pulled her close, "what is this business of mistakes and picking the wrong girl?"

"Well," she swallowed hard, "you have been withdrawn and spending more and more time away from here. I've tried to figure out what was wrong, but that's the only thing I could come up with," she finished with a shrug.

"Shew," Robert sighed, "well, I guess I have been withdrawn as you say, but that definitely is not the reason. I thought it would go away in time so I kept silent."

Micah's heart pounded. She wanted to yell that she had changed her mind and did not want to know. She knew in her heart what Robert was about to say was going to change her life forever and she was not sure she was ready for such a change!

"I'm not happy here," he continued. Micah's breath caught in her throat, terrified of what the next sentence might contain. "I was afraid it would break your heart and if not yours, then your father's," he hesitated, again. Micah could take no more. Now her father was involved!

"What! What is it!" she cried, "Tell me!"

Robert was slightly taken aback, but quickly put an end to her misery.

"I want to go west, to the frontier," he finished.

Air rushed from Micah's lips as his words began to make sense.

"I didn't want to say anything, but I want more than to live in someone else's abandoned cabin while farming my parents' land. I want my own land. I want to find it, claim it, and make something of it," he said, his excitement growing with every word he spoke. She had thought this was their home. He had spoken of building another house, but she had thought it would be here. Micah wanted to scream "No," but she held her peace.

"I haven't said anything because it would mean that you would have to leave behind all of your family and friends. I just didn't have the heart to ask you to give them up," he explained as his excitement overwhelmed him. "What do you think?"

"I don't know," she answered honestly, "I need time."

"Fair enough," he said, hanging the towel he had used on the peg. "Take your time and let me know when you have decided. Now, we have one more thing to set straight."

Micah looked at him with fear of the unexpected showing in her eyes. What more could he possibly spring on her in one day.

"This here business about me making mistakes and picking the wrong girl can't be left like that. I don't want you thinking this every time something seems to be bothering me. I didn't line you up or draw straws to pick a wife. I married you because I love you. Don't you think that if I had any interest in someone else I would have checked that out before I married you? I love you, Micah, and nothing is going to change the way I feel about you!" Robert pulled Micah into his arms and kissed her gently on the lips as tears of relief trickled down her face. Micah laid her head against his broad chest.

"Your supper's ready," she told him.

"It'll keep," he said, pulling her chin up so that she faced him, once again, and then kissing her passionately.

Micah spent almost every moment thinking about moving west. She wanted to stay here where she was now. She had never thought about living anywhere except here in this community. Robert had never mentioned any such dreams since they had met. Micah thought long and hard about the sacrifices she would be making by leaving her family so far behind and the fact that every time she thought about going west a feeling of warning welled up within her being. Yet, going west did spark her adventurous side. It was for this reason, coupled with the excitement that appeared in Robert's eyes and voice, that she kept her true feelings silent. Micah gave him the answer he wanted to hear about a week later.

"If you really want to go to the frontier, I will go with you," She told Robert.

"Micah, are you sure?" he asked, leaping from the chair he had been sitting in.

"I won't lie. I do not wish to leave my family and friends, but I will go wherever you want."

Micah had thought making the decision to go west was the hardest decision she would ever have to make, but she had been wrong. Robert had shared his desire for the frontier with no one. Telling the family, especially her father, was very painful. The outcome was always the same. It ended with tears from everyone present. There were those who tried to change Robert's mind and a few who encouraged him on his way. Micah had secretly hoped for the changing of the mind, but the decision seemed to be cast in stone.

The preparations for moving were now under way. The most pressing matter was the food that would supplement Robert's hunting game. Then they would need to take seeds for next spring's planting. They might get to plant a few things this spring, but with a cabin and animal pen to build, it would be wise to be prepared for the worst. Robert had no idea just how far he wanted to go, either. It may very well be that he would still be looking by mid-summer. Next, there were tools that would be vital to their success and survival on the frontier. The couple was faced with a dilemma of sorts. They would have to walk and haul their future on the back of the one horse Robert owned. This was not going to be an easy trip.

One evening nearly two weeks into the preparation Robert came home, beaming with anticipation.

"There has been a slight change to our plans," he announced. Micah raised her brow in question as she secretly hoped the slight change was his mind.

"Your brother and his family are coming with us. Now you won't be completely alone. I don't know how close we will settle, but maybe we can have an occasional visit from something other than a wild critter!" he grinned.

This was not what she had hoped for. It did make leaving home easier for her in one way, but worse in another. Now her father would be the lonely one.

"What about Pa?" Micah asked, concern showing on her face.

"Not to worry, Micah, he had already decided to return to Boston when we announced we were going west. And what's more is he's dividing the horses between you and your brother. Now you can ride and we will have another pack animal to carry more things. See, it's looking better already."

"Robert, how far west are we going?" she asked.

"As far as it takes," he answered, "I want to be on the very edge of the frontier. Maybe even push it a little farther west," he added with a grin. Micah mirrored his enthusiasm, but secretly the thought of going that far west struck terror in her heart.

Chapter 2

THE NEXT TWO weeks were exhausting both mentally and physically. Micah and Robert had their own preparations to deal with, but then her brother and father were both packing to move and Robert was trying to help his family and spend as much time as possible with them. There truly were not enough hours in a day. Micah actually found herself looking for the day of departure. It would put an end to some of the daunting craziness that surrounded the families.

The day did finally arrive. Everyone was packed, situated, or settled. Micah slid her arms around her father's neck and hugged him tightly. Tears ran down her face as sobs shook her tiny frame. She tried repeatedly to pull herself away, but her arms refused to let go. She knew deep in her heart this would be the last time she would see her father. Micah's father held her securely as he had many times before and let her weep. He had always been understanding and patient with her feelings. Micah believed God had given him a special gift in being sensitive toward her since her mother had died when Micah was so young.

"Robert, can you give Micah and me a few minutes together?" her father requested.

"Sure, it will give me time for one last stroll around the farm. Take as long as you need," with that, Robert left the cabin.

Micah's father pulled her toward his favorite rocker and seated himself, pulling her onto his lap. Micah's weeping continued as her father began speaking softly to her.

"Baby girl, we both knew this day would eventually come a callin' on us. Fact is, I knew it was closer than I wanted it to be the day you set eyes on that young man of yours. I remember," he chuckled, "the first day you seen him like it was yesterday. We went to see his Pa about buying this here piece of property and when we arrived at their house the men folk were out in the barnyard tryin' to break a young stallion. Robert, being the oldest, was getting to do the lion's share of breaking. I can't say how many times that he had been thrown, but he was covered from head to toe in mud and manure from a hard rain we had the night before. Now, my eyes thought it was the funniest thing I'd seen in quite a while, but you, with all that mud and smell could only see one thing: a young man that stole your heart. I knew then, it was only a matter of time before this day came knocking on my door." Micah's weeping had eased. Her father's soft, deep voice was soothing her aching heart as he took her thoughts back to that day.

"Pa," she sniffed, "I don't want to go."

"I know, baby girl, I know," he said, gently squeezing her in his arms.

"If I had known I would be leaving like this, I don't think I would have married him," she confessed.

"Baby Girl, I believe you would have and if you were honest with yourself you would have to admit that you knew he wanted to go west. When someone spoke of the land to the west there was a sparkle in his eye and a keen interest in his voice. Every time a frontiersman would come through or anyone with information about the land west of here, Robert never let his attention wander until he had gleaned every tidbit from them. His love for the frontier has always been there in the open. We both saw it. That's one of the reasons I insisted you wait until you were eighteen. I didn't think you were ready to face this day and I knew I wasn't ready to face my baby girl leaving for parts unknown. I'm still not sure I'm ready, but here we are."

Micah rested her head on his shoulder, still trying to quiet her emotions. "I thought I was ready for anything the first time I saw Robert, but now, like you, I am not so sure," she whispered.

"Aaaaah, Baby Girl, the truth is you've been ready for a good year. I've just been enjoyin' the time I still had with ya," he chuckled softly, "you're ready, but being ready doesn't mean it won't hurt to say goodbye. It just means there's love here," he said, patting his chest over his heart.

He was right. He always was.

"You're right, Pa, I just always pictured my life with Robert here. Our children would sit just like this on your lap and listen to you telling stories and now…," fresh tears stopped the rest of her words. Micah's father gave her time to calm her emotions.

"Micah,"

Micah's father had her full attention. He seldom called her by her given name. When he did, it was because he had words of importance to say.

"Micah," he repeated, "you know as well as I that this is the last time we will see each other."

She held her breath, trying to hold back a flood of tears as her father spoke her very thoughts.

"I have age against me and you will have distance against yourself, but time and distance can never stop love. You will be in my thoughts, in my heart, and in my prayers. Not one day will pass while I draw breath that I won't think of my baby girl and ask God to please watch over her. Now, you have a husband waiting for you that's most likely feeling very bad about taking you away. He's a good man, Micah, you chose well. I'm proud of you!" Micah's father carefully pushed her from his lap, stood, kissed her on the forehead, and added, "All little birds have to leave the nest. It's time for you to fly. Remember Isaiah's words, Micah, 'They that wait upon the Lord shall renew their strength; they shall mount up with wings as eagles; they shall run, and not be weary; they shall walk and not faint.' Fly like an eagle, Micah," then he kissed her forehead once more and, as he turned her toward the door, he tenderly pushed her forward and said, "you're ready, Baby Girl, I love you. Go with God," his voice broke as he finished. Micah turned to see tears tumbling down his time-worn face.

"I love you, Papa," sobs shook her slender shoulders as she stepped onto the porch and searched the farm for her waiting husband.

Chapter 3

THE DAYS OF travel were almost mind numbingly tiresome. The group walked up hills and down hills. Then back up and back down, again. The terrain was very steep and tree-covered. It would have been impossible for them to use the wagon. Robert and Micah were on foot with their belongings loaded onto three horses. Micah's brother had four horses with them. Three of the horses had been packed with goods as Micah and Robert's were, but the fourth carried his wife and infant son.

The destination of the small caravan was the western foothills of the Pennsylvania territory. The trip was breath taking in beauty. The trees were in spring bloom and a few flowers were cautiously pushing their tiny blooms skyward.

It was clear that Ben's wife Leigh had not shared Micah's hesitation about moving to the frontier. She bubbled joyously with each advancing step they took. Micah liked her and hoped that some of her enthusiasm would rub off onto herself. Micah could not imagine the frustration she would have succumbed to if Leigh had not been a positive companion.

They had scarcely made it down into the western foothills when Ben made an announcement during breakfast.

"We won't be going any further. We like it here. This is where we wish to make our new home."

"Are you sure?" Robert asked.

"Yes, we're sure. This is as far as we go," he answered.

"Would you like us to stay and help you put a roof over your heads?" Robert offered, as Micah secretly wished he would accept.

"No, if you plan to continue on you will need every day you can get to put a roof over your own heads. Unless you think you will settle nearby," he finished hopefully.

"No," Robert replied.

"I thought not. Take care of my little sister," he said, extending his hand, "Godspeed, my friend."

Micah said another tearful goodbye. The rest of the morning, the couple traveled in silence. When the sun stood directly above the trees, Robert turned to Micah.

"Do you want to stop and eat now?"

Micah shook her head, "I'm not hungry, maybe later."

Robert nodded. He knew her lack of hunger was caused by her saying farewell to what had remained of her family.

"Yeah, maybe later," he agreed as he sadly hung his head.

That evening, as they settled into their blankets for the night, Robert pulled Micah close.

"Micah, I'm sorry."

"Sorry for what?" she asked, as she pulled back and rose up on her elbow to face him.

"I knew that it would not be easy to leave everyone behind. I knew that it would be even harder for you, but I didn't know just how hard until you said goodbye to your father. Now, after seeing you say farewell to your brother.... I'm really sorry. When I see that sadness in your eyes I wish I'd never asked you to come here."

"Then I would be the one that was sorry," she said lying back down with her head on his shoulder.

"How's that?"

"Because, then I would be the one seeing the sadness in your eyes every time someone spoke of the frontier or every time you raised your head and looked to the west," she yawned, "now, go to sleep. Maybe you will find us a home soon."

"I love you, Micah. I'll find you a home soon enough, but for now," he leaned over her and kissed her tenderly on her lips.

When Micah began to stir the next morning, she could smell coffee and bacon. She opened her eyes to find Robert sitting by the fire, smiling at her.

"What are you doing?" she asked.

"Fixing breakfast. What does it look like I'm doing?"

"Well, fixing breakfast, but why?"

"Well," he mocked, "I figured that with all of the traveling we've been doing you could do with a little extra sleep."

"That's a very sweet thought my love, but as a general rule when fixing breakfast, the bacon tastes better if flames are not billowing from the skillet." she snickered.

Robert quickly pulled the skillet from the fire and put a lid over the skillet to smother the flame. Robert waited a few moments and then cautiously peeked inside the skillet. He looked at Micah with a sheepish grin.

"I hope you like your bacon well done," he grinned.

"Maybe you should cook until we reach our new home," Micah remarked.

"Why, do you think I'll know how to cook by the time we get there?" he asked.

"No. I think those hard black pieces of bacon would make nice shingles for our new home," she teased. "How are you at making oatmeal? We might be able to use it as chinking for the cabin walls!" she giggled.

"Well, if that's not a fine thank you," Robert said, putting the skillet aside and pouncing on Micah. He straddled her and tickled her until she begged for mercy, then he leaned forward and covered her face with kisses.

"You know," Robert said softly, "I am sorry your brother didn't come any farther with us, but I think I'm going to like all of this privacy that we now have."

The traveling continued until they were almost out of the western foothills. Robert had guessed they were fifty miles to the west of her brother's chosen homestead. Robert liked the land here and began to survey the area for an ideal spot for their cabin. One morning after breakfast, Robert went out in search of the perfect place. He returned about an hour later with excitement beaming from his face.

"I found it!" he said with breathless anticipation, "You'll love it! Come on let's pack up," he said quickly, packing and loading the horses as Micah extinguished the fire. They were on their way within minutes.

Robert took Micah to the north of where their camp had been. They followed the natural draw as it lay between the hills. Ten minutes later Robert stopped and pointed up ahead.

"There it is. See how there's a plateau around the hillside over there? We can build the cabin there on the backside. There is a creek that runs along the far end and about halfway down the field is a clear pool of water. The land here is rich and begging to be farmed."

Micah smiled. Robert's enthusiasm was contagious. Her heart pounded with excitement. She could picture their new home by the pool of water. It was beautiful!

"Come on," he urged, and they began to make their way around the hillside toward the plateau. The plateau was in fact a very large meadow that was breath taking. The little spring flowers were in full bloom in one huge carpet of blue, white, and yellow.

"Oh, Robert, can we build right here?" Micah said as soon as she reached the meadow.

"Well, we could, but you may grow tired of running around the hill to the pool for water," he grinned.

"Ohh," she groaned.

"I thought you would think that," he laughed, "We'll build small to start with," he said, taking Micah by the hand and walking toward the water pool with the horses, "then, as time allows and we need more room, we'll add on."

Micah smiled. Robert's desire for a family was as strong as his wanting to move west, but there was a feeling of relief that Micah was not yet expecting. It would be physically demanding on Micah as she helped to build the cabin and stable.

When the sun stood straight over head, Robert was looking at the completed lean-to that would serve as living quarters until the cabin was habitable. Micah had just finished the noon meal and offered Robert a bowl of food.

"After we eat," he said between mouthfuls, "I'm gonna start cutting trees for the cabin. The sooner we start, the sooner we finish."

"Well, at the rate you're going you will have the cabin finished by nightfall and be ready for an early grave," Micah stated.

Robert grinned, "I'll slow down when I get tired, but for now, I'm too excited."

"While you cut the trees, I'm going to unpack a few things and set up house-keeping in my new palace," she teased with an ornery smile as she nodded toward the lean-to.

"You do that, Queen Micah," Robert spoke over his shoulder as he walked away, "the king will return when he is hungry."

"Oh, wait," Micah said, "should I unpack the bacon shingles right away or will we not be needing them until tomorrow?" she asked with such seriousness that for a brief moment Robert thought she still had the charred pieces of ill-fated bacon.

Robert turned and leaped at Micah, but she was expecting such a reaction. She quickly side stepped him and began running. Robert gave chase and threatening to place the queen in the dungeon. Robert could most definitely outrun Micah, but making her laugh so hard she became weak made it a very short chase. Robert scooped her up into his arms, kissed her soundly, then tossed her over his shoulder and gave her a solid swat on the backside. This brought a squeal and laughter from Micah. Robert was now laughing so hard he staggered his way back to the lean-to where he gently placed Micah on the ground inside the shelter and laid down beside her. He lovingly placed a kiss on her forehead and played with the auburn hair that had worked itself loose and lay around her soft oval face.

A few minutes had passed when Micah asked, "Do you have that first tree cut yet, Mister Philips?"

"I don't believe the trees are going anywhere soon, do you?" he teased back, "I'm busy right now, anyway," he said, placing another kiss on her soft, pink lips.

When the day turned into night, Robert had cut four foundation logs and was in the process of dragging them to the site for notching and placement. Micah had unpacked and arranged, then re-arranged the lean-to until she was satisfied. The exhausted couple snuggled into their blankets, falling asleep immediately.

The next week went very much the same. Robert felled the trees and raised the cabin walls higher with Micah by his side. She stopped only to prepare food for them. They were developing a routine that seemed to flow well for them. Robert would rise at daylight and find fresh game for the evening meal. Micah would have the fire going upon his return with breakfast in the making and a supper cooking pot on standby in anticipation of Robert's return. Then Robert would take the horses from the picket line to the water pool to drink and Micah would fill the waiting cooking pot with Robert's catch. They would eat. Micah would clean the dishes while Robert would place two horses back on the line and bring the third horse to either the cabin site to pull logs up the skids into place or to the woods where Micah would hitch them to waiting logs. Robert would begin cutting more trees.

Each morning since their arrival a bald eagle would soar overhead and split the air with its sharp piercing cry. Micah welcomed the visits. It brought memories of her father and his final words. It made it seem like he was here with her in some strange way. Her visitor had yet to make his flight this morning.

A smile played on Micah's lips as her mind moved to a more recent memory of how her husband awoke her at dawn by pulling her close and smothering her with kisses. Her life seemed perfect. She was beginning to love her new home with each passing day. Her father had been right. She was ready. The land here was beautiful, she had a near-perfect husband, and the cabin walls would be up and ready for chinking by the end of the day. She was thinking about seeing if Robert wanted to just rest and relax tomorrow. She seriously doubted he would. He was more than a little bothered by the fact that they were at the mercy of the weather, wild animals, and whatever else might be lurking about the forest. It had been for these reasons he had risen at dawn and pushed until it had been too dark to see. He had notched more than a few logs by firelight

Micah dipped the shirt she had been scrubbing into the bucket of water to rinse. Robert had sent her to do as she wished. She had wished to do absolutely nothing, but clothes needed to be washed. Robert was notching the logs for the final layer in the cabin wall. He would call for her when he needed her to guild the horses as they were being pulled into place. The steady rhythmic ringing of Robert's ax reminded Micah of a waltz she would like to dance to, but she had yet to figure out a way for Robert to keep time with his ax and dance with her, too.

"Micah!" Robert shouted.

"That was quick," she said quietly as she stood to go help him. She had not taken her first step when she heard a high-pitched hissing sound from the woods behind her shoot past her and in Robert's direction. Before she could turn to see the source, she was hit solidly from behind and knocked to the ground. A frightfully painted Indian rolled her face-up and sat astraddle her with his tomahawk poised and ready to strike.

The warrior hesitated to give the fatal blow. Micah had heard of unimaginable horrors that had been unleashed by the hands of Indians. She did not know how much of what she had heard was truth and how much was a frontiersman's stretching of the truth, but she did not wish to find out first hand. If this was her time to die, she wanted it to be as quick and painless as possible.

Micah held the warrior's gaze eye-to-eye and said in a sarcastic tone, "Well, come on, show me the courage it takes to murder a defenseless woman. Show me the honor in sneaking up on me from behind!"

Micah had counted on the sneer in her voice to achieve her purpose. What she had not figured on was the fact that the warrior understood more than her sarcasm. He understood every word she spoke, as did some of the men with him.

A look of shock flashed in the man's eyes, but it was quickly hidden by dark anger. The anger Micah had hoped for. The time seemed to stand still as the man and woman stared at each other. Silence hung in the air with the tomahawk, and at that given moment the eagle's cry split the air as Micah's morning visitor soared over head. A slight smile of contentment curved Micah's lips. How ironic that her final thoughts would be of her father and his comforting words. The warrior raised an eyebrow to Micah's reaction to the eagle's cry. Then he ended the standoff with a disgusted grunt and slammed the weapon into the ground so close to Micah's head she could feel stray hairs being pulled out by their roots. Micah was jerked to her feet. She quickly surveyed the cabin area for Robert, but found no sign of him. Before Micah could complete her thoughts on Robert, a sharp pain shot through her head as her world turned dark. Her limp body fell into a heap at the feet of the man she had tried to goad.

"Why did you do that?" her attacker growled at the man who had given the blow.

"She's less trouble this way," was his reply.

"She was not being trouble. She could have walked, but now you can carry her," he said pointedly.

The offending man growled his dissatisfaction with the outcome of his actions, and then roughly threw the limp woman across his shoulder.

Micah's first comprehensible thoughts were of bouncing up and down with something hard jammed into her stomach. When she was finally able to open and focus her eyes, she was staring down at the back of buckskin-clad legs as they walked toward an unknown destination. The bouncing motion and the shoulder jammed into her stomach, coupled with the thumping in her head, made Micah nauseous. She groaned, and then vomited.

"She's awake now," the disgruntled man said as he threw her onto the ground with a thud.

Micah half-cried half-groaned as pain from the fall radiated through her body.

Micah's attacker walked back the line of men to the semi-conscious woman, took one look at her and said, "Not enough to walk."

"She just vomited on me," yelled the other man.

"You knocked her out, you carry her," the man retorted without any compassion for the other's plight, then turned about and continued on his way.

The furious man grabbed Micah by her upper arms and pulled her within inches of his own face.

"Do that again and I will cut your throat!"

The murderous tone and hate-filled eyes left no doubt he meant every word. Micah would have been obliged to repeat and put an end to her misery, but her stomach was empty. She was slung over his shoulder, once again.

Micah regained her senses enough to look for Robert. She twisted and peeked around the man to search the line of men at the front of the procession, but no sign of Robert. She raised her head enough to look behind them, no Robert. Her carrier gave her a repositioning toss and growled.

"Hold still or I will make you hold still with my war club!"

Micah's body went limp as a horrible, queasy feeling came over her being. If he was not there, he was still at the cabin. Tears silently splashed against the back of her captor's leggings and the ground beneath.

When evening came, the band of travelers halted. The seemingly endless hours of hanging upside down ended when the man let her body fall to the ground with the same pain-racking thud as before. Micah lay motionless for quite some time. She had not had a drink since this morning when she drank from the water pool while doing laundry.

"I need a drink," Micah stated.

The men around her did not even look in her direction. It was as if she had never spoken a word. Not sure of what to do, she sat where she had been dropped.

The man who had spared her life sat studying the young woman. He had every intention of killing her, but after the words she spoke, he could not do so without bring shame to himself in front of the very band of men he was leading. The outcome tore him. Many of the Indian nations were angry with the white settlers for sneaking over the mountains and taking land they had no right to take. There was a great deal of hate for them and the settlers that the war parties encountered were killed immediately or shortly thereafter. Most of the parties did not bring prisoners back to the villages. His band had intended to be prisoner-free, until this little wisp of a woman. He hoped she was strong in spirit and body for she would be paying the price for all white people who dared to cross the mountainous region and invade their home. Now her life would be a tortuous one to say the least, most likely her life would end soon after their return to the village. Her fate would be decided by the village chief.

Micah's thirst was maddening. She tried for a response once more.

"I need a drink!"

There was no response, just as before. The stream flowed just a few yards from where Micah had been so roughly deposited. She shakily stood to her feet. She took two steps toward the stream before she was grabbed from behind and thrown back to the ground, leaving her stunned and breathless. She blinked the tears from her eyes to see her tormentor was the man who had been carrying her. He stood over her with anger filled eyes.

"Be still!" he shouted at her.

"I need a drink!" she equaled.

"Be still!" he bullied through clinched teeth.

"I need a drink!" she equaled, again.

The man ignored her demand and walked away, believing his order to be final. Micah pushed herself to her feet, finding strength in the anger that now boiled inside. Micah took one last look at the man who still had his back to her and started for the stream. She had covered half the distance when she heard his thundering yell. The words he shouted were in his native tongue, but the tone said enough. She turned just as he grabbed her arm, jerking her around to face him, and slapped her solidly across the face. Micah was then grabbed by the other arm and yanked away from the angry man. Angry words filled the air, none of which Micah understood. Nor did she care to. Her goal at this point was to get to the water. Micah was fighting mad now as she turned her head to face her latest assailant. It was the band's leader. Anger burned in Micah's eyes as she met his gaze.

"I need a drink!" she said flatly. Both men immediately released their hold on her.

Micah took her time drinking. She did not wish to make herself sick by drinking too much too quickly. When she had her fill of water, she returned to the place she had been previously dropped. Stress, fatigue, and pain from the day's events left Micah exhausted. She curled up on the ground and went to sleep.

The leader of the group shook his head as a slight smile flickered across his lips. If this little show of determination was a sign of the run in between these two, the trip home would be more than interesting, and a healthy respect for this woman planted itself in his heart.

Chapter 4

MICAH WAS LITERALLY yanked from her sleep by a hand that wrapped itself in her waist-length hair that was now a ragged mess. She finally got her feet under her after dangling momentarily like a puppet. Micah was not surprised to find the offending hand belonged to the nasty man who had carried her yesterday. The instant Micah's feet were under her, the hand thrust her toward the stream. This continued until they reached the water's edge.

"Drink!" he commanded.

Before she could respond, the obtrusive hand caught the back of her head, pushing her to her knees and then thrusting her head beneath the water's surface and holding her there. Micah pushed, kicked, and flailed her arms trying to free herself. Then, as suddenly as the hand pushed her under water, it pulled her out again. Micah gasped, choked, and coughed, but before completely catching her breath, her head was pushed beneath the water's surface. When she was nearly unconscious, Micah was pulled from the water and dragged by one arm and her hair back toward camp. When her captor had returned her to her resting spot, he relinquished his hold and let her fall to the ground without breaking stride. He then returned to sit with the other men.

Micah was still trying to clear her lungs as she raised her head to see her captors were eating breakfast. Micah pulled herself upright and began pulling her thoughts together. Moments later, something hit her in the chest and fell into her lap. She looked down to find a piece of jerked meat had been tossed to her. She looked up at the group of men, all of whom sat watching her. Micah had no problem identifying who had tossed her the meat. The nasty one sat with a cynical smirk etched on his face.

Micah's anger began to grow. She understood very well that she had been tossed food like an animal. It was not until she retrieved the meat from her lap that she discovered the meat had been chewed on and still held the remains of excess spit. Micah looked at it with disgust as the nasty man sneered aloud. Micah's anger boiled hotter until rational reasoning escaped her. She shakily stood to her feet, approached the smirking man, then threw the meat striking him in the chest and landing on the ground in front of his cross legs. The cynical smile vanished. The insult now returned, Micah furthered the humiliation by turning her back to him and began walking away. This in itself was a statement. A statement that said she was not intimidated or concerned by him.

The man was upon Micah before she completed her first stride. He whirled her around, then slapped her to the ground, grabbed her by her upper arms, and lifted up her until her feet dangled above the ground. Her face was inches from his anger-seething face. He held Micah suspended in mid-air, staring at her with murder in his eyes. His chest heaved in and out as his body shook with the intensity of his anger, causing her body to tremble as it hung in his grasp.

The leader of the band stepped to the side of the enraged man and spoke.

"Remember, if you leave her unable to travel on her own, you will carry her."

"I will kill her and leave her for the buzzards!" he shot back.

"Then you will carry her dead body back. I said she is to be taken back."

The leader then turned in a westerly direction, leaving the angry man at bay and Micah still dangling in the air. The angered man released a frightful roar and flung Micah with all his might in the direction the leader had taken. Micah was knocked breathless.

The nasty one turned and retrieved his belongings. He wrapped his hands in Micah's hair as he walked past and pulled her to her feet and shoved her down the trail before him. The still stunned woman stumbled onward, letting her anger give her the needed determination to survive.

The procession traveled steadily throughout the morning. The hot sun beat down without mercy. Micah's "drink and refuse breakfast" left her strength wanting. She had begun to stumble more frequently. With each fall she was yanked to her feet by the most accessible body part; be it hand, arm, or hair, then shoved forward, again. The leader of the band never looked back, but was still aware of the events that transpired at the rear of the procession. He was surprised the young woman had made it this far. He could stop now to let the others eat and rest while she regained some strength and no one would be any wiser to the fact that he really felt pity for the little thing. When they reached a suitable place, he halted the men.

The party drank from the small creek, then found themselves a place in the shade of the towering trees and proceeded to pull food from their pouches and eat. Micah was roughly deposited at the base of a tree and left without food. When the men had rested and finished with their food, the leader stood, but before giving signal to go, he turned to the man in charge of Micah.

"Feed the woman," he said, pointing at Micah.

The man scowled and went to Micah, keeping his body between the leader and her. He handed her a piece of jerky the size of a half-dollar and yanked her to her feet. Then he turned to the leader and said,

"Ready!"

The leader frowned. He had his suspicions of what the man had done to carry out the order that had been given. This man was always disrespectful and rebellious. The fact that he was a very skilled warrior was the only reason this man was allowed to go on any war parties that he lead. When it came down to the facts, there were very few men he would trust with his own life. Any confrontation would only serve to agitate him and cause him to take his anger out on the woman. He would, for now, keep silent.

The travel resumed and Micah's strength escaped her, further. When evening came and they stopped for the night, Micah was to the point of collapsing.

Strangely enough, her tormentor took her to the water's edge and let her drink. Then he took her back to the group and pointed to a place on the ground for her to sit. She did as she was told and was handed a large piece of jerky to eat. A couple of men began preparing corn mush. When Micah had finished with the meat she was thirsty again. She stated she needed a drink and her captor nodded for her to go to the stream. Micah was completely confused by the sudden change in this man. She wondered at what had caused the new attitude, but at the same time, deep within her spirit, an awful feeling that something was terribly amiss clutched at her stomach.

Micah sat content among the men after she had eaten her portion of the offered mush and had satisfied her thirst once more. She closed her eyes and was trying to clear her mind of all thoughts when something landed in her lap. Micah opened her eyes and looked down at her lap to find a blood-matted clump of hair lying there. Micah wrinkled up her nose at the sight and looked up at the nasty one who had thrown it with questioning eyes. He smiled his evil smile as he squatted beside her, picked the clump of hair and turned it about for her to get a better look. A cold shiver ran down her spine as she realized that it was a human scalp! Her whole body responded to the sight. She stared at the man with horror frozen in her eyes. The man continued to smile his wicked little smile as he pushed the hair closer to her face wanting her to look once more. She did. Her stomach heaved instantly as the weight of truth fell upon her. The scalp was Robert's!

Micah rolled onto her hands and knees as her stomach heaved intermittently with her sobs until her stomach was once again void of food. She crawled a few feet from the vomit and fainted, face first into the dirt. Moments later, Micah returned to the world around her. As she lay on the ground, her body trembled with uncontrollable sobs that erupted from her shattered heart. The only recollection of the happenings around her was of one thing, the evil laughter that filled the air above her. Micah cried herself into a restless sleep only to awaken and relive the horrid incident, and cried herself to sleep again.

The leader watched the whole affair unfold. He had seen people tortured to death in many forms and had never so much as flinched, but the sight he had just witnessed ripped at his heart. Some of the men in the band laughed at the cruelty, but most, while their faces held no emotion, their eyes told the truth. They too, were torn by the devastation that had been unleashed on this young woman. He was comforted to know that some of these men had human compassion. This evening was the first time since she had been captured that she had really eaten enough food only to have this done to her. He quietly stood and walked into the woods where he could settle his own aching heart.

The next morning, Micah did not have to be awakened. She sat staring numbly, not knowing or caring about what transpired around her. When the band was ready to travel, the nasty one came to stand before her, kicking her to get her attention. He proudly patted the scalp that hung from a leather thong around his waist. His mouth twisted into a cruel smile as he looked down at Micah. Tears slipped down Micah's face as she turned away from the sight. He then gave a triumphant laugh as he jerked her to her feet.

"Drink?" he asked, mockingly.

Micah nodded, yes, without thinking.

She was half-pulled, half-dragged to the water's edge and given a drink. He held her head beneath the water's surface until she was almost unconscious. She was then pulled to her feet and turned toward the direction of the leaving group and flung headlong toward the other men.

"It would appear that Cold Water wishes to carry the woman again," the leader spoke without looking back.

Cold Water pulled Micah to her feet with a slightly gentler touch.

Micah stumbled numbly through the next two days, refusing any food or drink that was offered. She was on the verge of collapsing at the end of the second day. The strength that sustained her now was not her own, for she was completely spent. Her emotions were gone and her body was numb. She could not feel the earth beneath her feet or the small branches that tore at her arms and legs as she walked through the forest.

Running Otter, the leader of the group, studied the woman as the band made camp that evening. It was clear she would never make it to the village if something did not change. How she had made it this far astonished him. She looked like death waiting to happen. He was torn, once again, by the choices before him. The decision best for her would be to grant her a quick death here and now. What she would face in the village at the hands of many angry people would surely make Cold Water look like a sweet old lady! Running Otter knew all of this and still he wrestled with himself. He just could not give the death order. He could not even figure out why he wanted her to live. Was it because of the respect he had for the strength and courage he saw in her, or was it because he knew her death would bring such great pleasure to Cold Water? Whatever the reasoning behind letting her live, he went to the woman, pulling her to her feet, and taking her to the stream's edge. He gently pushed her into a sitting position.

He squatted beside her and looked into her eyes. Cold Water had succeeded. Her eyes were hollow and without feeling. Her face was pail with sunken eyes. She was not even aware of his presence. The day after seeing the scalp she had cried almost constantly. The second day she stared into the unknown. She had loved this man very much and Cold Water had found a way to kill her without taking her life. There was no honor in this kind of war!

"Drink," he said softly, "you drink now."

There was no response. Running Otter rose, walked a few feet behind her and stood leaning against a tree, pondering the woman's death. An eagle flew overhead and rent the air with its cry as Running Otter watched Micah. Running Otter raised his eyes, hoping to catch a glimpse of the bird. He was recalling that this same peculiar scenario repeated itself every time he was close to deciding this woman's fate. He heard a quiet sniffle from the woman.

Micah was looking toward the heavens and whispering, "Oh, Papa, Pray hard for me. I can't find the will to go on."

Running Otter squatted at the woman's side.

"Drink," he said softly, "you must or you will die."

This time, her empty eyes met his. She flatly replied, "I don't care."

"Well, someone cares. The eagle cries for you to live," he countered.

The words pricked at Micah's spirit. She sighed and drank water from the stream. Her empty stomach growled, gurgled, and groaned at the intrusion. When they returned to the fireside, she was given a bowl of mush.

"Eat slowly," he cautioned.

Micah did as she was told. She finished her mush and lay down, falling into a deep slumber.

Micah was greeted with another bowl of mush when she awoke in the morning.

As camp was breaking, Cold Water spoke. "Are we going to travel at an old woman's pace today?" he said with contempt in his voice.

"Seeing that it is your fault the woman cannot travel any faster, I would say we will travel at an old woman's pace, unless you would like to carry her at a man's pace," he added with a slightly triumphant smirk in his voice.

Cold Water let out a snort of disgust, but held his tongue. Several of the men grinned at the exchange of words. They had spoken in their native tongue, leaving Micah oblivious to the stinging words unleashed on the nasty man.

The next few days, Micah was given dried meat to chew as she traveled and allowed all the water to drink that she desired. She had become familiar with the routine of the group and knew just how far she could stray without getting herself into trouble.

One evening, after they had settled into night camp, Cold Water pulled a bottle of liquor from one of the packs he carried. It was among items taken from one of the homes they had raided. It did not take long for the man to become intoxicated. By hour's end he had finished the bottle and was passed out on the ground amongst the stolen goods.

The thought of how this wretched man would feel in the morning brought a smile to Micah's lips. I'd like to… she did not finish the thought. She was ashamed for even thinking such a thing, but try as she might, the thought kept coming back. Micah carefully moved closer to the one of the warrior's knife that had been used to prepare tonight's meal and slipped it into the folds of her skirt. She innocently wandered near the inebriated man. Micah stopped near the head of the man, stooped and quickly selected one of the locks of hair that were scattered about the man's head, pulled the knife from the folds of her skirt and removed a lock of hair about ten inches in length.

She had been undetected by everyone except one, up to this point. Running Otter would have been caught off guard, but for the fact he had been watching the woman at the time. He marveled at the cunning and smooth movement of the young woman. One of the other braves started toward Micah, but Running Otter stopped him. Micah smiled triumphantly as she held the lock of hair up for all to see as she put the knife back where she had found it. The stunned group of men stared in shocked silence for a brief moment then burst into laughter. Running Otter approached her as he retrieved a leather cord from his pouch. When he took the hair from Micah, she submissively held out her hands, fully expecting to be bound for her actions.

"No," Running Otter laughed.

Micah looked at him questioningly, but he only smiled. She watched as he took the cord and tied the lock of hair securely, and then tied the lock of hair about her waist so that it hung like a scalp from a warrior's belt.

"Good scalp, warrior woman," he grinned.

The camp erupted with mock war whoops, shouts, and outright laughter.

When morning came calling, Cold Water looked as if he needed to be carried. Micah had cut the lock of hair from the crown of the head. She had left approximately eight inches of hair still intact. Every time the hungover man bent forward to vomit, the lock of hair would fall into his face. Cold Water would push it backward only to have it fall where it had previously hung. Micah giggled at the sight and the men watched with laughter dancing in their eyes. Some smiled openly; she was surprised no one gave her away. The nasty man was too beside himself to discover her secret.

Cold Water glared at her for he knew this white woman was enjoying his misery. He decided he would deal with her, later, and then he vomited again.

It was not until they stopped for the evening camp that Cold Water noticed the lock of hair tied about Micah's waist. She had just walked past him when he stepped forward and grabbed her by the arm, swinging her around.

"What is this?" he growled at her. Micah only smiled at him. This puzzled him even further.

"What is this?" he repeated as he looked at the men about the camp.

Running Otter broke the silence, "It looks as if she has scalped an enemy."

"Enemy. When?"

"I believe it was while you were sleeping with the white man's bottle." Running Otter answered.

Cold Water was bewildered. Micah pulled free of his grasp and continued on to the stream to wash the day's dust and sweat from her face and hands. She was returning to the camp area when Cold water went to the fire and stooped to get a piece of roasted meat. Once again, the tattle tail wisp of hair fell into his face. He pushed it back only to have it return. He repeated the gesture. The outcome was the same. A look of shock froze on his face as he realized the meaning of Running Otter's words, and the hair tied around the white woman's waist. Cold Water roared with anger as he leaped at Micah, knocking her to the ground.

Running Otter had expected such a reaction and was ready. His only surprise was how long it had taken the man to figure it all out. As Cold Water sat astraddle Micah, he drew his knife from its sheath. Running Otter grabbed Cold Water from behind by his hair and placed his own knife at the angry man's throat.

"I will kill her!" hissed Cold Water.

"You will not," Running Otter countered. "I told you as I did all of the other men who obeyed me not to take the poison water when we raided the English. If you had not disobeyed me, you would still have all your hair. Just as the woman faces the pain of her man's death every day when she sees his scalp hanging from your belt, you will face your shame hanging from her waist. If this woman can face her loss surely a great warrior such as you can take the pain of a few missing hairs. Touch her and you die!" That being said, he released Cold Water.

Micah did not understand the words, but she knew the nasty man wanted her death with every beat of his heart. She also knew the leader had prevented her death. Micah smiled. Death would have been fine with her, but her living was a thorn in this man's side. Micah knew she should not feel delight in such knowledge, but she did.

The travel continued over the next couple of weeks and Micah became more familiar with the people who held her captive. She moved about the camp with liberty.

There was very little to do when they stopped at night, so Micah had made a habit of helping gather firewood. It was on one of these ventures that she found a feather from the breast of an eagle. Micah was instantly surrounded by memories of Robert, her father, and home. Comfort! It had been a very long time since she had felt comfort. Micah tucked the feather away in her waistband. She returned with the wood and went to the stream to wash up.

Micah lay back on the soft, moss-covered ground after she had finished with the evening meal. She lay with one arm under her head like a pillow and laid the other across her stomach. Something tickled her arm. Her first thought was another bug, but she quickly remembered the feather. She removed the feather from her waistband, twirling it by the sharp point. She was admiring the way it glistened in the firelight when it was snatched from her hands. Micah's response was instant. She was on her feet.

"Hey, that's mine!"

"Mine now," sneered Cold Water.

"Give it back!" she demanded.

Cold Water dismissed her with a grunt and walked away.

"That is my feather. I found it and I want it back!" Micah stood with her hands on her hips, determined to get the feather. Cold Water ignored her demands. Micah's face reddened with anger. The feather was her connection to home, her father's words, and the eagle that flew over the foothills every morning, but more than anything she needed the softness of its touch. It held the tenderness of her father's voice, and the gentleness of Robert's hands. This wilderness only held harshness that until now, she never knew existed.

"Give it back!" she repeated through clenched teeth with a vehemence that brought Cold Water's attention back to her.

Micah knew his physical strength outmatched her, but her favor with the leader by far outmatched his. If she had a chance of getting the feather back, it was Running Otter. Micah, angry and determined, marched up to Running Otter with her hands on her hips.

"I want my feather back. I found it while gathering wood," she pleaded her case.

Running Otter sat slightly stunned, once again, by the grit and determination of the young woman.

"The feather is hers. Give it back."

"She is a white woman," he hissed, "and this is an eagle feather!"

"I know what she is and I know what that is. The feather belongs to her," he repeated, "if you want the feather, trade her for it."

"Trade!" exasperated Cold Water. "Since when does she deserve to be traded with?"

"When she scalped you," he answered.

Shock and shame covered Cold Water's face. Still holding the feather he asked, "What do you wish to trade for the feather?"

Micah, hands still on hips, gave a disgusted gasp. Her gaze was locked onto Cold Water's face. He was not going to get her feather.

"You have nothing I want," she said with flippancy, then quickly snatched the feather from his grasp before he could reply.

The humiliated man reddened with anger as he clenched his teeth and fists. He whirled about and stomped into the woods to pout.

Running Otter stood with no evidence of emotion on the outside, but inside he was hiding a grin that would have covered his face from one ear to the other. The smile of triumph that curved the woman's mouth as she watched the beaten man stomp away made him turn quickly away to busy himself with a meaningless task to keep his smile hidden. He chuckled quietly to himself as his respect for the woman grew. Then, as quickly as the chuckle sounded, it was silenced by the grim reality of her end plight. He may not have found the strength to end her life, but the anger and hatred that awaited her would surely call for her tortured death. Silently, he pleaded with The Great Spirit that it could be different for her. High in the sky a cry rang through the air. The cry carried itself to the earth and touched Running Otter's ears.

Running Otter whispered, "Call on my friend. I want her to live, too." The saddened man sighed as the eagle's cry faded from hearing.

Chapter 5

THE REMAINDER OF their trip was filled with weary travel. First, they traveled uphill, and then down, only to repeat the process again. When they were not going up and down, they were crossing creeks, stream, or rivers. Cold Water approached her several times, trying to get the feather; he was, of course, unsuccessful in his quest. The rest of the time he avoided her as if she were not there. This arrangement suited Micah fine.

The group stopped one afternoon to eat and rest as they usually did, but Micah sensed something was different. The very atmosphere around her seemed to shift. After lunch, the men began to disappear then reappear freshly bathed. While most of the men had been quite clean, there had been a couple of them that did not seem familiar with all of the uses of water. Micah's stomach began to churn as the men began to reapply the war paint that had been present the day they had fell upon her and Robert. Many of the men had washed the paint from their bodies a few days after the attack. A couple had let it wear off, but for the past few weeks the paint was gone. Micah prayed hard there would not be another raid. She had become relaxed among these men after so many weeks of travel. There had even been a friendship of sorts with them. Now that the paint was back in place, Micah was reminded of who her captors were. A chill ran down her spine and uneasiness settled over her as she shuttered. Micah made her way to the leader of the party who was painting his face in the same horrifying pattern as when they first "met".

"What is happening?" she questioned as she knelt beside the man. He stopped painting and stared momentarily into the woods. He turned to face Micah.

"We are home. Tomorrow we enter the village. The runners have gone ahead to tell them of our arrival." His gaze held eye-to-eye with Micah a moment longer, then he returned to painting his face. Micah searched the half-painted face for a clue to what was causing the unrest in her spirit. His eyes and face held just a trace of sadness that gripped at her heart and caused the uneasiness to be more intense. Micah walked away from the group and sat at a distance with her back to them. She could feel what little connection she formed with them slip away. She would face what tomorrow brought alone. Micah prayed.

When morning came, the men had their paint back in place. It was both shockingly beautiful and horrifying. Vivid yellow, green, blue, vermilion, and black intertwined from head to toe. No two men were alike in color or design. The return of paint hurled Micah back from her false sense of security so that the very air she breathed was filled with a chilling awareness of danger. Micah shuddered visibly again.

Running Otter sat quietly as the rest of the men laughed and joked with one another. Normally he would have been in the middle of the jesting, but as happy as he was to be home, his mind was overshadowed with regret. It had been a great raid. The men had burned seventeen cabins and killed all of the inhabitants. No one in their war party had been killed and the only injury was not caused by a battle, but while they were traveling. One of the braves had fallen while walking along the rim rock when it gave way. The man had fallen about fourteen feet and broke his arm. "Correction," he thought. They had killed everyone except for this woman they had started calling Little Eagle. He would delight in telling of the battles one-by-one and the many daring and brave deeds of his men, and how the enemy had cowered at the very sight of them. He did, however, wish he could dismiss himself from the events that awaited this young woman. He smiled as he thought about the pleasure it would bring him to recount the stories surrounding her and Cold Water. Many men cowered at the sight of them stepping from the woods, but not this woman. She had shown strength, determination, and guts, even in the face of Cold Water. He would speak of her in a positive light in his retelling, but he was sure her spirit would speak for itself when the time would come. Running Otter sighed. If he had just killed her when he had the advantage, she would not be facing the most trying and pain-filled time of her life. The man sighed again, and decided he would not feel guilty. Running Otter resigned himself to the fact she would die soon.

Little Elk had been sitting next to Running Otter, seeing the focus of his gaze and hearing the sigh. Did Running Otter have feelings for this woman? Little Elk searched his friend's face. No, he did not believe this to be the case. Running Otter, as well as the rest of the men, had acquired much respect for this woman and did not wish to see her death. Cold Water's hate for the woman was overshadowed by the respect he had for her strength. Little Elk placed a hand on his friend's shoulder. Running Otter turned to face Little Elk. Neither spoke a word, but understanding pasted between the men.

The men, now satisfied with their appearance, journeyed on toward the awaiting village. As their destination grew nearer, excited chatter erupted from some. Others were lost in thought. Micah was one of the latter. She paid little attention to anything that surrounded her being. She needed help that only God could give and Micah was well aware of this fact. It was an uneasiness she felt. The unknown she sensed. Her focus was on God and God alone. Micah's attention did not waiver until she smelled smoke.

One of the men moved to her side and began the process of binding her wrists with a thong of leather. Micah gasped in horror and disbelief, but said nothing. He stared at Micah in silence for a few moments. He looked toward the village then back at Micah as if he wished to say something. Still, he remained silent. Just before he turned toward the village, Micah saw something in his eyes that made her blood run cold and caused her to swallow hard at the tears threatening to escape. It was there in his eye for a fraction of a second, but there nonetheless.

His eyes had said, "I'm sorry."

Running Otter nodded for Micah to move in the direction of the village. The procession was within sight of the village in moments. People were calling, running, greeting each other as the arriving party reached the village. Instantly, Micah was pounced upon by women and children slapping, hitting, spitting, and kicking. An unknown attacker bit her at one point. Solid smacks brought tears to her eyes. Balled fists in her mid-section caused her to bend forward. Sharp toes made her side-step first to the left, then to the right as the spit splattered, ran, and dripped from her face and hair. Micah was too shocked at first to respond. It was not until the hate-filled face of a woman stood only inches from her own, screaming words that held no meaning, that anger gripped her temper. Micah balled her fists without a second thought and swung upward with full force under the woman's jaw. The connection was solid. The woman staggered and slumped to the ground with a thud. Micah stepped over her and continued with the group of men who seemed to think the matter was not worth stopping for. The once pressing crowd made sure there was a safe distance between them and her. The attacks still came, but they were fewer and a little less severe as the women and children danced in and out hitting, spitting, and punching. They were making a game of her misery, playing out the actions of a warrior when they count coup against an enemy. The happenings around Micah were a loud, pain-filled blur. The hand of a warrior squeezed her upper arm and pulled her through the crowd of people. She was able to comprehend that the hand belonged to Cold Water with deliberate concentration. He led her to a place where three poles were set erect in the earth. She was tied to the center pole. The men that had been her captors moved away from where she was tied. The majority of the village followed the men. There were a few women and children that remained where she had been tied. Micah still was on the receiving end of an occasional blow, but for the most part the tactics changed. A small group of children came toward her with a handful of creepy, crawling creatures, mostly spiders, and placed them in her hair and down her blouse. She did her best not to show any response to the crawlers. She knew from experiences with her brother that if she reacted to this with fear or disgust, the longer this would continue. The children began to wander off within minutes. The response they looked for was not to be found at Micah's expense. Micah sat like a stone wearing a smile, but on the inside it was all she could do not to turn into a screaming, wailing maniac. She could feel soft, tickling feet, hard, grasping, and clawing feet, mingled with an occasional bite. The remaining watchers soon became bored with her and went about their way.

The return of the warriors was cause for celebration. There would be food, dancing, and an account of the warrior party's exploits. The village was in a buzz. It had been from the time runners brought news of their arrival. The village had readied itself for the arrival and the celebration that was already on the verge of being in full swing.

Micah had been stood against the front of a pole with her hands tied around the pole behind her back. Micah could stand up, sit down, bounce, and shake, but that was the extent of her abilities for movement. She took advantage of the privacy the bored onlookers left her. She did her best to shake, wiggle and bounce to dislodge any insect that had not found its own way out of her clothing. When she was satisfied she had done her best, she slid down the pole into a seated position. Micah leaned back against the pole and closed her eyes. The pain and exhaustion from her welcome to the village consumed her body.

She was thinking strongly about trying to maneuver herself into a prone position when a sound or presence caused her to open her eyes. A young boy, about six years in age, with a rueful little grin on his dirt-streaked face stood before her with something concealed in his little hands. The boy boldly approached Micah, pulled up her skirt with one hand and tossed something onto her outstretched legs then let the skirt fall back into place. The unknown intruder immediately began to scurry about, looking for a suitable hiding place. Micah could take no more. She kicked and struggled trying to stand and remove the unwanted intruder. She finally made it to her feet and jumped up and down a couple of times, which caused the creature to roll out onto the ground at her feet. Micah was both relieved and shaken as she watched a large spider that equaled the size of her hand with its extended legs run for cover. The little boy and his audience of interested followers squealed and giggled with delight to see Micah's performance. Micah visibly shuddered as the nasty creature disappeared beneath a small pile of someone's belongings. Micah watched the little boy run to several adults, point to her, and regale them with his deeds. He was openly praised with words, smiles, and a few pats on the back.

"Such fine parenting," thought Micah, "he nearly gives me heart failure and they give him a 'good boy' pat."

As Micah watched the boy telling one after the other, she started to smile, then giggle with the little fellow. The ornery little thing was just like her brother when they were younger. Her brother would catch nasty creatures and put them on her or chase her with them when they were younger, then he would announce the deeds to the world. Micah laughed out loud and shook her head as she sat back down and leaned against the post.

The large area that seemed to be the center of the village was littered with eating, laughing, and talking people. The food smelled wonderful! Micah's stomach growled with hunger as she watched the celebration. A woman with food in her hand finally started toward Micah. She was sorely disappointed when she realized the woman had come to retrieve the pile of belongings that her "pet" spider had hidden under. The woman lifted the parcel and the frightened spider ran as fast as its eight legs could go right up the woman's leg. The startled woman jigged sideways while flinging the parcel and stomped her foot. She dislodged the spider with her first stomp and squashed it with the second stomp. The woman snatched up the bundle and gave the spider a glancing grunt as she walked away. Micah did not believe the woman was afraid, just caught off guard. The happening made Micah giggle. She wished she could give the little boy a good boy pat! The spider's fate was a pleasing one to Micah, only to be over shadowed by a small truth Micah understood. The chances of that being the last large spider around here were very, very slim.

Micah longed for just a small morsel of the food that scented the air around her, but much to her dismay she received nothing. The attitude of the village was like that of the men who attacked her and Robert. The slight friendship and acceptance that had grown between herself and her captors was now gone. She expected no kindness to be shown. Her welcoming party was proof of that frightening fact.

The village inhabitants began to congregate in the open area around Micah after they had filled themselves with food. The villagers sat encircling the poles where she sat bound, leaving a distance of approximately twenty feet between themselves and her. Micah swallowed hard at the panic threatening to erupt in the form of tearful sobs. She managed to hold herself together by the grace of God. The band of warriors that had captured her sat in the front row to the left and a group of men whom she figured to be men of position in this village sat in the front to the right. Running Otter stood halfway between the seated people and herself. He faced the people, raised his right hand and complete silence followed. Running Otter spoke at length as the listeners sat spellbound by his words. He was met with gasps, awes, laughter, and nods of approval. The leaders and listeners alike ignored Micah. The lack of interest in her by the village gave Micah a feeling of ease. She was beginning to think the man would never stop talking when the tone and topic of the conversation shifted. All eyes appeared to be shifting back and forth between herself and Running Otter. Micah could follow some of the conversation by the hand gestures the man used to tell his story. The imaginary raised tomahawk, for instance. When Running Otter began to gesture between her and Cold Water, her nerves began to fray. He was indicating Robert's scalp that hung around Cold Water's waist. Micah was sure that with the thoroughness Running Otter had given this trip so far, her revenge scalping would not be left out. She was right. The next subject started with Running Otter drinking from an invisible bottle, followed by many words and hand gestures that ended with pointing to the hunk of hair that hung tied about Micah's waist. Running Otter's method of talking, mixed with the motions and hand gestures, and acting out of the events, held his audience captive as he gave a detailed account. Micah watched Cold Water's face as Running Otter told the story without prejudice for either person. Cold Water's face was like stone; A stone that was etched with humiliation and scorn.

The listeners responded with shocked silence and then found the whole affair quite entertaining. There were mock war cries, shouts of triumph, and open admiration for Micah in the face of her enemy. Cowardliness in anyone was detestable. Bravery was admired and not taken lightly.

The subject changed and Micah was relieved she no longer seemed to be the object of Running Otter's continued account. Running Otter stepped closer to Micah moments later and gave the eagle feather in Micah's waistband a little flip with his fingers. This too, was met with nods of approval from her captors.

Running Otter's speech continued and Micah began to relax once more as the attention had been diverted from her. She was feeling somewhat dazed by the sound of Running Otter's voice as he continued with retelling their raiding trip. Micah was pulled back to awareness when Running Otter's voice stopped. Hundreds of eyes were staring at her, and a man Micah would guess to be chief stood and took position beside Running Otter. The silence seemed to be endless and Micah's spirit churned. Something was brewing. Micah swallowed hard as she tried to rid herself of the uneasiness. Micah watched the people around her, hoping for a clue. What she saw caused the upheaval inside of her to become even greater. They, too, were watching the two men that stood before her. The village sat poised and ready. *Ready for what?* She wondered.

The silence continued as the man beside Running Otter stared at her as if he could see right through her being. It was clear the man was contemplating a decision he considered to be of great importance. Micah knew in her heart what the decision was, but she searched Running Otter's face, hoping she was wrong. Running Otter had been staring, stone-faced, over her head at first and then made full eye-to-eye contact with Micah. His face never betrayed his emotions, but his eyes, for a fleeting moment, silently apologized. Micah visibly jerked as if an invisible hand slapped her when the reality of the situation struck home. That man was deciding her fate.

A torrent of emotions passed through Micah. The fact that this man dared to think he had the right to decide who lived and who died was no small irritation to Micah, but on the other hand, she had wished for death ever since the moment she had heard the thud of Cold water's war club steal Robert's life. Oh, how she wanted to die right here and now. She did not want to be here in this horrible place one more moment, but the Spirit of God that lived inside of her compelled her to get up and live every day.

The whole village seemed to hold its breath in anticipation. There were two people who did not: Micah, who was gripped by fear of the unknown, and Running Otter, who feared what he considered to be the worst.

"God in heaven, have mercy on me," she quietly breathed.

The words had no meaning for the man who held her fate, but Running Otter heard and silently agreed.

The silence was shattered when the elderly man standing beside Running Otter made a brief statement. The village turned to total chaos. It had the appearance of an anthill that had been kicked. It took only a few moments for a method to the madness to become clear. Shrieking women and children ran away from the area, only to return armed with large sticks or war clubs and form two parallel lines. Micah was befallen by several women who removed her bindings and began pulling and tearing at her clothing. Micah fought with all her might, but was stripped completely naked within minutes. Micah stood in stunned silence, trying to cover her body.

Running Otter stepped forward and stood in front of her. Micah opened her mouth and tried to speak. No words were found as she helplessly shook her head 'no'.

"You will run the gauntlet," he stated as he held her gaze.

"What?" the still too stunned Micah tried to comprehend.

"You will run the gauntlet," he repeated. "You must go from here," he said, pointing the end of the line that was closest to her, "and run to there," as he indicated the other end of the line of eager participators. "If you do not make it, you will begin all over. If you cannot go again, you will die a death of shame."

"And if I make it?" she questioned.

"That is not for me to say," he answered.

"I die anyway," she sneered through clenched teeth, "why bother to run at all?"

"You will die a death of shame," he returned.

"What's the difference? Dead is dead!" she hissed.

"Death with honor is quick, without pain. A death of shame will be long and painful," he finished, stepping aside as another man took her by her forearm, leading her to the beginning of the waiting line.

"Quick and painless," she decided.

The hate-filled cries rose to a deafening pitch. A hand from behind Micah roughly shoved her into the waiting lines. She was met with several blows that caused her to stagger and hesitate. Micah could faintly hear Running Otter's voice yelling for her to "run" over the cries of the crowd. Instinct took over and Micah snapped into action. She had made three quarters of the distance when she was tripped. The lines converged on her beating, kicking, and spitting. Micah tried repeatedly to get up, but could not move. Amidst the beating and kicking she became aware of the reason she was unable to get up. One of her attackers had their butt firmly planted on her mid spine. Micah seethed with anger.

"Not fair," she screamed.

The craziness of the situation struck Micah and she began to laugh intermittent with moans and cries from the blows she received. There was absolutely nothing fair about any of this. She was being beaten and hated for something she did not understand, by people she did not know, and did not even play by their own rules. They were beating her to death and her last grand statement was "no fair". Now, Micah was about to be done in by someone's big butt.

The crowd began to quiet and step back. Micah assumed they were checking to see if she was still alive, but it would not be hard to know otherwise by her mixture of moans and giggles. Micah could see men's moccasin feet standing beside her. The butt that still sat atop her was dislodged with one quick motion and lay sprawled in the dirt with Micah. This only made Micah laugh more.

"Oh, no," Micah giggled to herself, "I wonder if being conquered by a butt is honorable?"

Hands grasped Micah's upper arms and pulled her to her feet. She was carefully pushed in the direction of the beginning of the line. Micah groaned as she realized they were going to make her run again. Anger began to take over her emotions. When she reached the front of the line her tormentors let her catch her breath. They were toying with her like a cat plays with a mouse. Here she stood, naked in front of God and everyone, dripping and oozing blood from cuts and welts that she received from an angry throng of women and children. What was it Running Otter had said? "Quick and painless." Micah boiled. How could anyone hold a straight face and say this was quick or painless?

Running Otter had been watching Micah's expression as she stood there waiting. A slight smile curved his mouth as he saw what he had been hoping to find. It was the same anger and determination he had faced the day he had taken her captive. The same was present when she repeatedly faced off with Cold Water. He could see it in burning her eyes now. She would take no more of this without a fight.

Micah had focused on Running Otter's face and seen the smile curve his lips. She mistook the smile as proof he was enjoying her misery. Her resolve deepened as her determination set itself in stone. Micah would not let these people be her defeat. She sprang into action before anyone could push her into the waiting lines. The tormentors were caught off guard by her actions. Micah made one third of the distance before anyone could react and land a solid blow. The war cries were deafening once again as she fought and pushed her way forward. Most of the blows she was receiving left her stinging, but the few that were direct hits were starting to take their toll on her body. Micah was turning blood-streaked and smeared to the point of not being recognizable. A sickening feeling began to sweep over her. She did not think she was going to make it this time either, and she knew a third time was out of the question. As quickly as the thought flickered through her mind it was replaced with sheer rage. Micah's body stiffened, her hands clenched, she half growled, half-screamed throwing herself forward, once more. A woman about three inches taller than Micah stepped forwards and blocked her path at the same moment. The woman was wielding a club that she held in front of her chest in a horizontal position. Her intentions were to catch Micah across the chest and push back in the direction she had just come.

Micah's momentum had peaked when she made contact. She caught the weapon with her hands, pushing the club up and back into the woman's face, spraying blood over both women. Micah's body crashed into the dazed woman, sending her back onto the ground. Micah leaped and sidestepped the sprawling body. She stumbled as she was clearing the downed woman. She spun about, trying to regain her balance. Micah could hear the whack and thud of wood striking wood. It was then she saw that she still held the club in her hand and she had been instinctively using it to block many of the blows. Micah brought one end of the weapon up with her right hand and caught an unsuspecting woman along the side of the face. Blood spilled from the woman's cheek and ran down her face. Micah began to swing her club about with no particular aim. This caused the lines to back away to a safer distance and widen her path. One woman was undaunted by the weapon she carried and stepped forward to stop Micah. Micah deflected the blow with her club then quickly flipped the stick around and rammed the end of it into the woman's unprotected gut. The woman folded as Micah pushed past her in anticipation of her next challenger. There was no one in front of her, but she received a solid shove from behind that sent her sprawling into the dirt, tearing the flesh on her hands and knees. Micah sprang to her feet as fast as she went down.

The war whoops and cries had reached fever pitch as Micah turned about, looking for an attacker. The lines of village woman and children had raised their weapons, but no one struck her. She had reached the end of the lines and they were saluting her.

Micah dropped to her knees as she tried to catch her breath. Two men grabbed her by her upper arms, and pulled her back to her feet. She was taken back to the pole where she had been previously tied. One of the braves started to bind her wrists.

"No!" Micah said flatly.

The young brave stood poised and blinked his surprise. He stared momentarily into Micah's dark, angry eyes. He quickly grabbed at her wrists once more. Micah was ready and escaped his grasp as she hissed.

"I said no!" she whirled about to face the now quieting crowd. The only noticeable movements were the loose whips of hair that were gliding on the breeze.

Micah had intended to march her battered body right back to the chief, but stopped after her first step. He was only ten feet from her and quickly closing the gap with Running Otter close behind.

The chief spoke to Running Otter, who started to translate, only to be cut off by Micah. She glanced momentarily at Running Otter's anxiety-ridden face. Micah locked eyes with the chief and began to speak.

"I have been dragged here over hills and streams. I am so far from home that I have no hope of returning and not once did I give you reason to tie me. You've stripped me naked and beaten me half-senseless for no reason other than your pleasure. Now, I refuse to be bound again. I will stay here," she said pointing to the pole, "Until I am told to do differently. Now, can I have my clothes back?"

Running Otter had begun interpreting when she finished her first sentence. He finished and stood silently, watching her with uncertainty. Her straight-forwardness, coupled with her fiery determination, had been an object of admiration up to this point, but Running Otter now feared she had crossed the line with Talking Mink. Her gaze was steadfast with the chief. He had seen some very nervy men fold under the chief's gaze. Talking Mink would often use this tactic to see how movable or unmovable a person was on a matter. Micah never once indicated any sign of dropping or shifting her resolve.

Talking Mink could go either way. He might see her actions as disrespectful, or he could decide it was pure courage. It would be a very fine line with Talking

Mink. The village stood motionless, afraid any movement might cause them to miss what came next. Running Otter's stomach quivered as he read the chief's body language. He was not going to respond to the woman's outburst, but he was going to pass sentence on the woman. Her fate was decided.

"The woman will remain here," he said, indicating the pole, "for three sunrises. Anyone wanting to claim her as a family member or a wife may come before council and give reasons for this right. If she is not claimed by nightfall on the third day, she will become a village slave. It will be as she has said. She will remain here and not be bound. Give the woman her clothing." Talking Mink nodded to Micah with a smile creasing his tired old face. Then he turned and walked away.

Running Otter, too, turned and walked away; releasing the breath he had been holding. He knew she would be fine now. Her wounds would be cleaned and dressed by some of the village women. The women would see to it that she received food. His mother, being the kind person she was, would most likely take it upon herself to see that every kindness was shown to this woman. Running Otter's heart was now light. This woman was no longer his responsibility and things were working out well on her behalf. He was finally home. He figured she would be claimed before nightfall. It was their custom that anyone in the village who had lost a family member had the right to claim her to replace that member. Those whom most commonly claimed captives were the elderly that had no one else to care for them. Next in line were those replacing a wife and then you had men just looking for a wife. His worry with this woman had ended. One thing was for certain. This experience would always be in the back of his mind when he was involved in future war parties. He had truly expected for her to be put to death, but now the ending had been pleasant. He smiled, even chuckled, as he pushed Micah from his thoughts.

He eagerly replaced them with thoughts of another young woman. The woman he intended to take as his wife at the harvest moon celebration. Two and a half more moons and he would have someone to warm his cold winter nights. It was not uncommon for some men to take more than one wife, but Running Otter had taken his time searching for the right woman. One woman would be enough if she were a good match.

He had seen men take more than one wife and everyone seemed to meld into one big happy family. This was not the usual outcome of most multiple arrangements. The constant fighting and unrest was unbearable to those around these people. Then there was the fact that, given enough time, a few of these families would reproduce to the point the husband could not feed them all and then the village would have to step in and help support and care for the children.

Summer Breeze was beautiful. Hearing her voice made him forget things. Her beauty was breathtaking and turned him to clay. No woman had ever stirred his blood like Summer Breeze. She had to be the one for him. It was like she was with him wherever he went, making his hair dance or the fringe on his clothing sway on a gentle breeze.

Running Otter's smile broadened and his steps quickened. He had spied her up ahead, making her way through the lodges with water containers.

Micah's wounds had been cleaned and dressed, and food was brought to her just as Running Otter had predicted. Her clothing was returned as she had requested. The clothing had suffered much damage. The blouse was ripped down the front from neckline to hem. Her skirt was torn only part way down from the waist. Micah tied the edges as best as she could and was able to keep herself covered. It was not pretty by any means, but it was sufficient.

Chapter 6

WHEN MORNING CAME, she found herself to be very sore and stiff. One of the women that cared for her the day before returned and motioned for her to follow her. Micah complied. The woman led her to edge of the village where some bushes were located. The woman stepped to the backside of the shrubs and squatted down and relieved herself.

"Oh," Micah understood and did likewise.

The two women walked back to the pole in silence. The woman went over Micah's body, checking her wounds. She reapplied salve to the wounds after which the woman disappeared for a few minutes then returned with food for Micah. Then the woman left Micah to herself. Well, to herself if you did not count the fact she was on constant public display in the center of the village.

The first day she seemed to be quite the point of interest, but as time passed she began to lose her popularity. Micah used her time contemplating what would happen next in her world. She had made her stand on being bound. The old man said his piece. Then everyone went his or her way. Running Otter had said nothing to her before he walked away.

One theory she imagined was that they were waiting for her to die, but that did not really work because they were feeding her and caring for her wounds.

Micah's worst case scenario was that they were making her well enough to play another game with her that was more horrid than the previous gauntlet.

Her nerves were beginning to fray after the second day of not knowing her fate. She watched for a glimpse of Running Otter among the lodges. If she ever laid eyes on him again she had some questions for the man. She and Running

Otter had not talked much when they were traveling, but now she spoke to no one.

Running Otter had slipped just close enough to the center of the village to see if Little Eagle was still at the prisoner poles. Two days had now passed and she was still there at the pole. There was talk around the night fires about her being claimed as a family member or some young buck's woman, at first. The talk was still heard, but now it was usually about her being a village slave. The thought of her being a slave was sickening to Running Otter. There were very few people he would wish slavery to be their fate. While Running Otter was walking about the village lost in his thoughts, he passed close enough for Micah to spy.

"Running Otter," she called, "Running Otter!"

Running Otter grimaced and approached rather hesitantly.

"When are they deciding my fate?" she quizzed.

Running Otter raised his eyebrows. It was not until now that he realized he had not translated. This would have been easier had he done this in the beginning. The outlook had a positive ring to it, but now two days later, things were not as positive. Running Otter took a deep breath.

"It has been decided." he said, ignoring the shocked look on her face. "You are to remain here for up to three days. Someone from the village may adopt you or you may be claimed for a wife. If no one adopts or marries you, you will become a village slave."

"Those are my choices?" she gasped.

"Not your choices. The people's choices," he corrected.

Running Otter saw Micah's body stiffen as anger flickered through eyes. He turned and began walking away.

"How many days has it been?" she called.

Running Otter stopped and turned to face Micah.

"Two," he stated and walked away.

Micah was livid. She could not believe that crazy old coot could come up with such an unbelievable sentence. The one outcome of adoption was the only one she thought would be acceptable, but wife, she would rather be a slave then to be bedded by some strange savage! Micah vacillated between outright rage and being insulted, only to return to anger with herself for being insulted.

That night found Micah still ranting to herself about the situation.

"How dare they just choose my life for me?" she hissed. "Leaving me out here like yesterday's garbage because I am not good enough for your family!" she pouted.

The predawn hours found Micah grateful that Running Otter had not translated on the first day. Three days and two nights of this torture would have been unbearable. She was going to need more strength than she could ever manage on her own. She needed God's help. That might not be so easy. She had been angry with God lately and she feared God may not be very happy with her as well. Micah began looking at herself and her situation. She had to get her life back into perspective. If any help came it would be from God. She was alone. There was no one else. Tears began to spill for the first time since the days immediately following Robert's death.

Micah was not the only one who lay awake, bothered by the future she might be facing. Running Otter lived in a community lodge with ten other families. Each family had their own separate living quarters. His living quarter was the second on the right from the center of the village. He and his mother had taken up residence here just after his return from the raiding party. They had moved there in anticipation of his upcoming marriage to Summer Breeze this fall. She lived in the last section on the left. It would work out well, she would marry him and move to his quarters and still be in the same community lodge with her family and friends. That would be a plus in many ways. In times when he was away or when their children were born, she would have plenty of help and company at hand. He quietly sighed as he pictured her in his mind: her large brown eyes and soft smiling lips and her laughter floating on the air. Running Otter stared at the twinkling stars through the smoke holes in the roof. Slowly, the face in his memory began to change. The eyes were not dark brown and smiling, but green and sad. There was not a soft smile on the lips and the laughter was silent. It was the face of Micah. The face she would be wearing as a slave. A slave's life was horrid. It was so horrible that he himself would prefer death. He was sure Micah would feel the same if given the choice. Someone would claim her. There was still time.

The third day at noon, Running Otter could not believe she was still at the poles. She was an excellent woman. This was going to be such a waste. The people of the village had seen her worth and the men in the raiding party witnessed her courage first hand. He knew the hatred for the English was strong, but his people believed there were good people among their worst enemy. Running Otter went about his day, debating with himself as to why she had not been claimed.

Micah had awoke the third day feeling stiff and numb. The smell of smoke from the morning cooking fires mingled with the scent of pine. She had spent yesterday shuttering at the faintest thought of being taken against her will to the bed of a total stranger. Now she was facing the future of a life as a village slave. She had watched a man who seemed to hold that title in the village. Slave life was brutal and that was sugar-coating the matter. She wished her fate had been death. Why had she been spared for such a future? Was God really that angry with her? Micah wanted to pray, but she could not find any words. She wished the sun would never set on this day, but wish as she did; the sun followed its usual path across the sky. As the evening shadows lengthened, Micah dropped her head to hide the tears that streaked her face. It was decided. She was defeated.

Overhead, an eagle gave its forlorn cry. Micah sobbed as the memory of her father flooded her thoughts. How she longed to sit on her father's lap and be rocked as he gently smoothed her soft hair. She longed to smell the scent of Robert. Washed or sweat drenched, she did not care. Just so it meant she was not here, just not here. Micah tried hard to control the sobs that were erupting. She managed some control, but for anyone paying attention it would have been easy to see she was crying.

One person had noticed and it was Running Otter. Three days ago he would never have believed that she would still be sitting by the pole. The day was ending, and Talking Mink was coming to give further instruction on carrying out her sentence. From the sadness in Talking Mink's eyes, Running Otter figured the old man thought she would be claimed before now, too. A few interested people gathered to watch Talking Mink make the sentence final.

Micah was pulled to her feet and turned to face Talking Mink. The old man winced at the wet trails that streaked her face. He took a deep breath and readied himself to speak, but exhaled after a few moments. He hesitated and then set himself to continue. Running Otter knew he would not hesitate again. As Talking Mink's lips parted to speak the first word, a quiet voice spoke, "I'll take the woman."

It was not until Talking Mink looked at him like he had lost his mind that Running Otter realized the voice had been his own.

"You?" Talking Mink asked.

It was public knowledge that Running Otter and Summer Breeze were an item. It was understood that Running Otter had been a firm supporter of a man being devoted to one woman. Now, two and a half months before the expected marriage, Running Otter does this.

Running Otter's silence was taken for a firm decision, but the truth was that he was the most uncertain person here and he was speechless. The faces around him held shock and surprise, but none more than his own face. There was one face in the crowd that held much more. It was the face of Summer Breeze. Running Otter only caught a quick glimpse of her face, but it was enough.

Talking Mink grunted, nodded, and dismissed the matter of Micah as he walked away, leaving her in the care of Running Otter.

Running Otter turned his attention to Micah. She stood with a terrified expression frozen on her face. "Come" he commanded as he turned to lead the way. Micah followed as new tears retraced her face.

Running Otter took her to his lodge quarters and told his mother to "make her a bed. She will be staying with us."

"We have responsibility for the slave," she stated, unsurprised. He was responsible for bringing her to the village so she would become his burden. She was taken aback by his response.

"No," he said flatly.

"No?" she asked with raised brows.

"No," he repeated and left the lodge.

Running Otter's mother stared after her son in disbelief, her mind bombarded by questions without any sensible answers. She knew her son's desire for a one-woman marriage. She had supported that completely. His fascination with Summer Breeze was apparent, but she secretly hoped he would see through her fake self. She was beautiful on the outside, but quite the opposite on the inside. She had seen evidence that Summer Breeze had a black heart. She had prayed often for The Great Spirit to open Running Otter's eyes to see her evil. Still, his eyes could only see her outer beauty.

Mother snapped out of her thought world and began to plan a reset of the lodge layout. Not much would change. She would make room for the woman on her side of the fire pit.

Micah still stood where Running Otter had left her. She found this to be the strangest slave arrangement she had ever seen. The old woman was working with a purpose while she stood idly by and watched the whole reset. When the woman finished making a place for Micah to sleep, she turned to her and pointed to the bed and said one word. Luckily it was one Micah had learned well during the trip here. She had been told to sit.

Micah sat on her bed, watching the woman putter here and there as if she were distracted and not really concentrating on her tasks.

Micah had waited for further instructions, but received none. The lodge had become too dark to see and the woman went to bed. Micah did likewise.

The comfort of Micah's bed held her captive until day light was well under way. The old woman was moving about the lodge, gathering supplies to take outside so she could prepare food over the outer fire pit. A fire inside of the lodge would cause unbearable heat in the lodge this time of year. Micah sat up and then followed the woman outside. She was not sure what was expected of her, but she had decided as a slave she would be a co-operative one, maybe even submissive.

There were a few women already around the fires preparing food for their families. Micah thought most of the staring would be behind her now, but found all eyes were on her once again. How interesting could slave life be? Things must have been very boring around here lately, she thought.

Mother had noticed the eyes upon Micah and found it very rude. She placed her supplies by one of the logs used for seating then turned to Micah.

"Come," she said, then turned and walked toward the woods. Another word she understood. She obeyed. The woman began gathering firewood when they reached a heavily wooded area and Micah followed suit. It was universal knowledge that if you wanted a hot meal, there was firewood to be collected. Their

arms now full of wood, they returned to the fire. The eyes were a little more re-
spectful, but it was replaced with an attitude of nonexistence. They were ignored
completely. Mother found this to be just as rude, but Micah preferred this to the
staring eyes.

Mother made quick work of the corn mush and berry mixture. When the
food was finished she told Micah to come and went inside the lodge to eat.
Mother was in no mood to eat her breakfast with such people. This was, however, not her only motive for going inside. Summer Breeze was due to make her
late morning appearance. Just exactly what Summer Breeze's reaction was to the
turn of events concerning this woman was a mystery, but the chances were that it
would not be a pleasant one. Summer Breeze had made several comments about
how special she was, so special that her husband would never want a second
wife. Mother thought postponing the meeting as long as possible was probably
the wisest thing to do.

Micah took the bowl of mush Mother handed her and the two women ate in
silence. When they had finished, the woman took the bowls and started outside
to clean them in the river. Micah rose to follow, but the woman told Micah to
stay. Micah, feeling very much like a trained dog, obeyed.

Mother had formulated a plan while they ate. It would be too dark inside the
lodge for them to do much without a fire and it was too warm for an inside fire.
There were cooking fires at both ends of the long house and she would see which
fire Summer Breeze had decided to use this morning. The other fire was closer
and more convenient, but many times she had chosen the fire on the opposite
end just for the purpose of getting close to Running Otter. She and Little Eagle
would make their getaway in the opposite direction.

Mother had decided that until she could clearly communicate the thought
"this is Summer Breeze, she would like to slit you throat for taking her man,"
she would avoid Summer Breeze if possible. Truth was, she would have avoided
her anyway.

Mother found it all clear at their end of the long house. She suspected that
Summer Breeze was still sulking about Running Otter's claiming of the woman
and was not quite ready to face anyone yet. If Summer Breeze had been any other
woman, Mother would have felt sympathy for her. What did cause her concern

was the evil Summer Breeze would unleash on her and the unsuspecting white woman when Running Otter would wed Summer Breeze. A cold chill ran up Mother's spine and made her shiver at the thought.

Mother put the bowls away and quickly gathered her pouches and told Micah to follow. She led Micah away from the prying eyes of the village and found a shady spot. She and Micah settled down on the soft, moss-covered ground beneath the trees.

Micah watched as the woman removed leather, rawhide string, and tools from one of the pouches. Micah understood very little of what this woman was saying, but she knew she was being taught the art of making moccasins. The Indian woman was a patient teacher.

After a while, Micah's stomach began to grumble and the woman opened another pouch and pulled out two chunks of dried meat. Micah took her piece and lay back on the welcoming moss. She found this woman's demeanor to be relaxing. Micah knew nothing about this woman except that she liked her. The women ate their food and continued to rest in the shade.

The woman picked up the moccasin Micah had been working on and examined it carefully. She nodded approvingly and laid it back down and rose from her resting place.

"Come," she said to Micah. Micah stood and began to gather their things, but the woman stopped her.

"No, come."

As they walked, the woman began pointing to the things around them and said the names then waited for Micah to repeat. Half an hour later, they found a thicket of raspberries. Mother quickly produced an empty pouch for them to fill with berries. Micah surmised that this woman had lived here all of her life and probably knew where every berry thicket was located in a ten mile radius. She was only half right. The woman knew where most things could be found, but she had not lived here all of her life.

The older woman started back in the direction of their previous place beneath the trees where they had worked the moccasins. They gathered their things and continued their leisurely stroll toward the village, repeating language lessons as they walked.

It was early evening when they made their way through the long houses to the one that contained their lodge. The older woman picked up the pace until they slipped into the darkness of their lodge.

Micah was told to sit once more as the woman left the lodge. Micah sat in silence and listened to the village sounds. The main sounds her ears picked up were barking dogs and laughing children with an undertone of voices both near and far. She began trying to piece together what was happening in her own world. Running Otter had told her that she would be a wife or a slave and she was still there when the old man had returned, but this was not what she was expecting slave life to be like. She had caught a couple of glimpses of a man that she was sure was a slave. His clothing hung in shreds from a half-starved body. He worked hard and received what seemed like routine lashings. Here was most likely as it was anywhere else. You had good and kind masters and then there were masters who enjoyed the misery they caused in another person's life. Micah gave a prayer of gratitude for the kind master. Maybe God's grace was still with her. Her anger with God had been on an increase since Robert's death. If she were to be completely honest, she had harbored a slight agitation in her heart toward God when she had left her family and gone with Robert. Now she found herself praying and pleading with God one minute and accusing Him of not caring the next. One thing she did believe was that being given over to this kind woman was one of God's mercies and for this she gave thanks.

The kind old woman re-entered the lodge and broke into her thoughts. The woman was carrying two bowls of steaming food and was followed by another older woman carrying a third bowl of food. Micah was given a bowl of food and the two women sat down to eat.

Running Otter's mother, Yellow Moon, sat beside the unused fire pit opposite from her longtime friend, Dragonfly.

"Where is Running Otter?" she asked.

"I do not know," she answered, "I have not seen him since he brought the woman here."

"Summer Breeze is in a black mood," her friend stated.

"Summer Breeze lives in a black mood," she returned.

Dragonfly laughed and then became serious, "Watch out for her. She is seething with black anger."

Yellow Moon nodded again. "I wish Running Otter could see the evil in her," she commented, "I am afraid the woman will wish for death before Summer Breeze is finished with her," she said nodding toward Micah.

Micah finished her food then stretched out on her bed and listened to the hushed tones of the two women's voices and the village sounds as her thoughts began to drift. It was not until Yellow Moon took the empty bowl from Micah's hand that she woke and realized she had been sleeping. Micah bolted upright and began wording an apology. Yellow Moon patted her shoulder gently and shushed Micah. Yellow Moon and the other woman took the dirty dishes and left Micah sitting in the lodge. She was trying to shake the sleep from her foggy mind when she realized she was not alone. Micah's eyes focused on the face sitting on the other side of the fire pit.

"Running Otter," she said with surprise. "The woman you gave me to is very nice. I thought slave life would be much, much worse than it has been so far. She's really..."

Running Otter cut her off. "You are not her slave. She is my mother and you are my wife."

"No!" Micah stated emphatically. Running Otter's expression remained stern and unchanging. "You said that I would be a slave if no one claimed me."

"And just before the chief branded you a slave, I claimed you."

"Why? I don't want to be a wife," she cried.

"I know, but this is better..."

"Better!" she cut him off, "Better for who? You?" she asked with a sneer. Micah was on her feet now, as was Running Otter. They stood face-to-face as Micah's eyes flashed her anger.

"I can give you back to the village as a slave if you want, but know this; as disgusting as you think being my wife will be, being a village slave will be even more so."

"How?" she shot back the heated question.

"As my wife, you go to my bed and only my bed. As a slave, you will go the bed of any man who wishes to have you. Slave women don't last long. Slave men get their share of beatings, but women…" Running Otter stopped speaking. The expression on Micah's face told him he had made his point clear. "I will let you think about what you want. I will give you the choice, but know this, if you choose to be my wife, I will expect you to be my wife in all ways," he finished.

Micah gasped and backed away from Running Otter. After a few moments, Micah sat down and stared blankly into the unused fire pit. She broke the silence. "You said the woman is your mother?"

Running Otter nodded and sat back down on his bed, "her name is Yellow Moon."

"She is kind. I like her," Micah commented, trying to make conversation. She was not sure which was worse; the awkward silence or the fear of him returning to the previous subject. Micah understood she had been given a choice, but she wished to delay her answer as long as possible. "All this time I thought I had the best master anyone could hope for," Micah spoke her thoughts aloud.

"She would not have treated you any differently if you were her slave. My mother shows only kindness. She doesn't even take part in the gauntlets. It is her way," Running Otter praised.

"More of you should take lessons from her," Micah snipped, but Running Otter let the comment pass.

"I will ask for your answer tomorrow," Running Otter said as he stretched out on his bed and closed his eyes.

Micah already knew what her answer was going to be, but she was hoping to get more than a day to put it off. Night had fallen and Micah still sat staring into the darkness. She could not cry, think, or pray. She felt empty and lost. Her father and Robert seemed like a dream from a lifetime away, but it had only been about two or three months ago. Micah no longer existed. She was Little Eagle now. A silent tear ran down her face as she gave a sigh of surrender. She had fought hard to remain Micah, but that woman was dead like her husband, Robert. Little Eagle curled up on her bed and waited for sleep.

The next day started pretty much the same as the previous one. Breakfast followed by a quick walk to their cozy moss bed beneath the trees. Micah had one of her moccasins done and was very close to having the second one ready to wear. She was a little excited about her new shoes. She had been barefoot the day she was taken captive and she still was. She made the trip here without shoes. Little Eagle was startled when Running Otter suddenly appeared before them. His mother just smiled.

Running Otter sat down with the women and picked up the moccasin Little Eagle had finished. "Good work," he stated. "When I was a small boy, my mother would go into the woods and wait for me to track her. She said it was good practice for a young hunter." He smiled. "You have my answer?"

Micah had to separate who she was from the person she had to become. She could not be Micah and be this man's wife. Robert was gone, but she would feel she had betrayed him if she kept any connection to her previous life. Micah could not bring herself to say she would be his wife so she nodded and said, "I will be Little Eagle." She felt like she had just renounced her love and devotion to Robert. The squeezing in her chest seemed to be suffocating her. Little Eagle tried to lift her gaze and look the man in the eye, but was too ashamed.

"I will give some time to adjust, but I will come to you one night," he said softly. Running Otter had watched her facial expression and heard the tone of her voice as she spoke. Her spirit was broken. He had saved her from devastation only to single-handedly crush her by his actions. This was not his goal. He was not in love with this woman, but he did like who she was. "I will trade for doe skin so you and Yellow Moon can make a dress. I do not want my wife in torn clothes," he finished with a forced smile and disappeared as quickly into the underbrush as when he first appeared.

Little Eagle sat still, staring at the ground before her. She had not responded to anything Running Otter had said. She just stared and trembled.

Yellow Moon pulled two cornmeal cakes from a pouch and gave one to Little Eagle and began eating the other cake. Little Eagle nervously played with the cake, but never took the first bite. Yellow Moon encouraged her to eat at first then she took the cake from Little Eagle and placed it back in the pouch. The older woman watched to younger one for a few moments. She knew what had just transpired between her son and this woman. Yellow Moon was torn. She knew her son was bothered that he had just broken this woman, but this could work out for the best. It would make him a little more sensitive toward Little Eagle as she learned her new way. She also understood the feelings and emotions

Little Eagle was experiencing now. Yellow Moon had not come here willingly. It took a couple of years before she was able to look back and see any good memories. She truly hoped this young woman would be able to find the good things that were happening at this time. Yellow Moon stood up and said, "Come" to Little Eagle. A quiet walk would be better than sitting and staring.

Yellow Moon let her walk in silence for a few minutes then started playing the word game of what things were called. Little Eagle did her best to be a good participant, but she was still clearly distracted. The two women made their way back to the shaded, moss bed where they left their belongings. Little Eagle sat back down in her spot and picked up the moccasin she needed to finish. She held the shoe only moments before she gasped in disbelief. She turned toward Yellow Moon and handed her the moccasin. The sole of the shoe had been cut from heel to toe. The shoe was ruined. Yellow Moon quickly grabbed the other moccasin. It too had the ugly cut from end to end. Little Eagle could take no more. Tears began to run down her face and before long sobs were trying to erupt. Yellow Moon moved closer and put her arms around Little Eagle. Little Eagle fell against the woman and sobbed. The motherly love and compassion that flowed from this woman was a soothing touch she needed.

Yellow Moon understood more than words could ever reveal. She stroked the young woman's hair and let her cry. She knew it was more than ruined shoes. It was the release of emotions from the loss of a man she had loved and a way of life she held dear. It was being made a captive and then being given to a stranger and told you would be his wife. It was hard and cold. Yellow Moon was sure this would not be the last time this young woman would need a shoulder to cry on. She did wish she could tell her it would get better with time.

Chapter 7

The next couple of days went as they had been going, rushing out in the mornings and remaining away from the village most of the day, only to return to the lodge, eat, and go to sleep. The only change was when it rained most of the third day and they stayed inside the dimly lit lodge. Little Eagle noticed that Yellow Moon was doing her best to keep her away from the other people in the village. She had been trying to reason why. Was it because she was ashamed of the fact her son took a white woman as his wife? There was turmoil between the two races and now would not be the ideal time to do this. Or were the tensions so high that the people of this village would not be very kind to her or maybe even toward Yellow Moon. After all, she was the mother of a man who had a white wife. Little Eagle wished she knew the ways of the people she now lived with. It would make things so much easier. If the opportunity presented itself, she would talk with Running Otter this evening. Running Otter had honored his word thus far and was giving her time to adjust before he consummated the marriage. She was grateful for every day that passed, although she was sure that he could give her ten years and it would not help the way she felt about being another man's wife.

This morning Running Otter would be joining them for breakfast so they went out to eat by the fire. There were a few curious eyes, but for the most part, no one noticed them and she felt like she blended in with the rest of the people. This feeling lasted until a pretty young woman approached the fire. She was tall and willowy with an air of confidence and self-satisfaction. There was marked tension in the gathering with her arrival. It was most noticeable in Yellow Moon.

The young woman ignored Little Eagle for a few minutes then made eye contact with Little Eagle. Her face was expressionless at first then she smiled at

Little Eagle. Little Eagle stared at her momentarily then gave her a faint smile. Little Eagle shuddered slightly. The smile on this woman's face was one of beauty, but there was evil in her eyes. Little Eagle felt like she had just smiled at the devil himself. Yellow Moon handed Little Eagle and Running Otter a bowl of food and began to eat her own quickly. Little Eagle followed suit. She was eager to get away from the woman with the evil-filled eyes.

When they finished cleaning and putting away the breakfast bowls, Yellow Moon and Little Eagle made their way through the lodges until they came to one with a woman outside scraping a deer hide. Yellow Moon called out to her. The woman turned and greeted her company with a wave and a smile. It was the woman who had come to their lodge just after Running Otter had claimed her. The two women quickly exchanged pleasantries then Yellow Moon took the flat rock from the other woman. Yellow Moon turned to Little Eagle and motioned for her to come closer and watch. After demonstrating how to use the rock to scrape the hide, she handed the rock to Little Eagle. Yellow Moon watched her for a couple of minutes to make sure she understood. When she was confident that Little Eagle could handle the job, she and the other woman went into the lodge and left Little Eagle to scrape the fat and flesh from the newly stretched hide.

A short time later the two women reappeared with hides that had already been tanned. Yellow Moon and Dragonfly approached Little Eagle. Yellow Moon held one of the hides up to the front of Little Eagle and Dragonfly held one up to her back. Little Eagle stood with her arms held out to the side and still holding the rock. The two women measured and marked the hides and then left her to her scraping chore.

Yellow Moon and Dragonfly found a comfortable spot on the ground in the shade not far from where Little Eagle worked the hide.

"Summer Breeze came to the fire this morning," Yellow Moon told her friend.

"What did she do?" Dragonfly asked. Her eyes were large with fright.

"She smiled," Yellow Moon said.

"Smiled?" repeated Dragonfly.

"Running Otter was there," she explained, "she's not about to show her true self with him sitting there." Dragonfly nodded her head in agreement with Yellow Moon.

"I am glad you could help me with this dress. Little Eagle needs to know how to make a dress, but she needs clothes now. She is inexperienced and it would take days for her to get it done. Running Otter wants her out of the rags she is wearing and in a decent dress as soon as possible. With the two of us working on it we can have her in one by nightfall. Thank you for your help," Yellow Moon said. Dragonfly merely smiled and patted her longtime friend on the arm.

It was just as Yellow Moon had said: Little Eagle had a dress. It was not fancy, but it was well made and ready to wear. As Little Eagle removed her tattered clothes and slipped into the new doeskin dress, she felt the tiny bit of her being that still clung to the person of Micah disappear from her body, soul, and spirit. Tears welled up in her eyes. She felt as if she had just witnessed her own death; A death that had gone unnoticed by everyone. The person Micah Phillips died and there was no one to mourn her. How could God just forget who she was and where she was? How? These were the questions that nagged at her daily.

Yellow Moon sensed her despair and slipped out of the lodge to give her time alone. She knew Little Eagle was grateful. She had smiled and thanked her when she presented her with the dress. She had been sincere. This was not where this young woman wanted to be. Yellow Moon understood that the changing of the clothes held a symbolic meaning for Little Eagle.

That evening when Running Otter returned to the lodge, he was pleased with her new dress. He complimented her and thanked his mother for making it so quickly.

"Running Otter," Little Eagle began, "is there a lot of turmoil in the village over you taking a white woman for a wife?"

Running Otter raised a questioning eyebrow and answered, "No, why?"

"I just wondered" she said losing her courage, "with the war between our people I thought the village might have a problem with me."

"When someone adopts or marries a person from another tribe or race they are not seen as an outsider. They are one of the tribe. You are now Little Eagle, one of us," he explained.

Little Eagle nodded her understanding. He had meant for these words to be an explanation of comfort and confirmation, but they were like salt in an open wound, and they magnified the feelings of non-existence in which she was already drowning.

The talk with Running Otter had left her feeling more confused than ever. Why all of the seclusion if she was no longer an outsider? This morning's breakfast was the most public exposure she had had since she was on display at the post. She was off to the side of the village when she was scraping the hide at Dragonfly's lodge. Yellow Moon was a kind and gentle woman. Little Eagle knew there had to be a reason for her to keep her separated like she had been doing. She purposed in her heart to learn the language quickly so she could ask for herself. The roundabout way of gleaning hints through Running Otter only served to make her more miserable.

Little Eagle's seclusion began to fade with time. She spent more time with others in the village. Her life began to take on some semblance of a daily routine. She was helping with chores instead of following Yellow Moon around like a lost puppy. Little Eagle could even communicate with limited language and hand motions with others. The summer heat now drove many inside the cool dark lodges for relief. Others chose relief in the cool river water.

Running Otter ended the adjustment period and claimed his rights as her husband. He had been gentle and undemanding. He had held her for a few minutes afterward then left her alone and returned to his own bed. Little Eagle held her composure until she heard his breathing change to his sleep rhythms. It was then that her body shook with silent sobs. Little Eagle felt Yellow Moon's hand brush the hair from her face as she softly said "shhh." Little Eagle grasped at Yellow Moon's hand. Yellow Moon took Little Eagle's hand and squeezed it lightly while Little Eagle buried her face in her pillow and cried herself to sleep.

Summer was almost over and Little Eagle understood most of the conversations around her now. She no longer cried after Running Otter visited her at night, but she was still grateful for every night he left her alone. Yellow Moon had told her that the village would soon have its final celebration before the weather turned too cold. Yellow Moon has said there would be dancing, eating, and storytelling until late into the night, but Little Eagle sensed that Yellow Moon was nervous about the celebration. As sweet as this woman was, she could be quite strange at times.

A couple of weeks ago Running Otter had started taking Little Eagle on walks during the evenings. They did not go every night, but they would go every other day if the weather permitted. Little Eagle was actually enjoying the walks. Sometimes they talked and other times they just walked. It was usually Running Otter that initiated the conversation, but tonight she did.

"Yellow Moon told me about the fall celebration that is coming up," she began, "it sounds like fun."

"Yes, it is," he answered.

Little Eagle frowned. She had been hoping for a hint to Yellow Moon's nervousness. "Tell me about it," she encouraged.

Running Otter raised an eyebrow and took a breath. "There will be eating, dancing, singing, game playing, and storytelling."

Great, she thought, *he's no help*. Little Eagle decided that the direct approach might get better results. "Yellow Moon seems to be nervous about the celebration. Do you know why?" she asked.

"No… Yes, I might." He had been trying for two weeks to tell Little Eagle about Summer Breeze. His mother had been upset with him because he was still going to take Summer Breeze as his wife so soon after taking Little Eagle. Yellow Moon had been adamant that it was not fair to Little Eagle, considering the situation. Maybe his mother had been right, but he knew Little Eagle tolerated her situation because she had to. Summer Breeze would be his wife because she wanted to be. Why wait and have two disappointed women? Summer Breeze would be happy as his wife and Little Eagle would be happy because she was not the object of his attention. "Long before I brought you here I had chosen to take someone else as my wife. We were to be wed at the fall celebration," he informed her.

Little Eagle stopped and turned to face Running Otter both stunned and horrified. "Are you still…?" she asked in a barely audible voice.

Running Otter nodded *"yes"* to her unfinished question. "I have been trying to tell you for a while now," he told her.

"Oh, is that why we started taking walks?" she asked. He nodded again. "Well, I guess you won't have to walk with me anymore," she snapped as anger began to creep into her voice.

"Mother does not like my decision. She..." he started.

"I like your mother more and more every day," she said sharply then turned and quickly walked away, leaving him to stand alone. He was not quite sure what to think. He thought she would have been happy about it. This had not gone at all like he had thought or wanted.

Little Eagle had not gone far when she came to a sudden halt, turned around and went back to the still befuddled man. "Who is this woman?" she asked.

"What...she is called Summer Breeze," he answered.

Summer Breeze! Little Eagle gasped in horror and turned to leave again. Running Otter was ready this time and grabbed her by the arm to stop her.

"I do not understand," he said as he turned her around to face him. "I thought you would be happy that I would leave you alone."

Little Eagle was too busy being horrified about being in the same house as the woman with the evil eyes and being married to a man with multiple wives to have considered this. As badly as she wanted to scream that the woman he was about to marry was evil, she refrained. "This is hard for me. I was raised in a house where we believe one man, one woman in a marriage," she explained.

"You have until the fall celebration to adjust," he said matter-of-fact.

"Just the self-centered comment I would expect from a man," she snipped back. Running Otter met her gaze but remained silent. "I incorrectly thought that while we do not love each other, you were making an attempt to get closer to having a true marriage by taking me on walks and making a point to talk to me, but all the while you were just trying to get up the nerve to tell me you were replacing me with what you consider a better wife."

Running Otter stood silent. He was not sure what to say and he did not like what she had just said. "You should return to the lodge," he finally spoke.

"Gladly!" was her reply as she turned and walked away.

Little Eagle was so disheartened by this turn of events. This was most definitely not her idea of marriage. She had been thinking that she could adjust and find some form of happiness in this unwanted marriage. All of this time she had thought they were getting closer as husband and wife. She had pictured things going differently. She was sure she was carrying his child and was planning to tell him so. Now she would not tell him until it was evident. When she first became aware that she might be with child, she was somewhat detached from the idea as a whole, but now she felt rejected by Running Otter and the child she now carried became the one being that gave her a reason to go on. She would sooth her loss and emptiness with the coming of this child. Little Eagle had started to draw closer to Running Otter and was beginning to feel as if she was part his world. Now everything changed. With Running Otter taking another wife, she was once again a side show, an outsider. This second marriage would make it a permanent fact.

When Little Eagle returned to the lodge, she went to bed. She was in no mood to make nice with anyone and tears were threatening to spill at any time. She wished for a secret place where she could go and be alone, but this village was so large with people going and coming, she had not been able to find such a place. It did not help matters that Yellow Moon never let her out of her sight, either.

God, her heart cried, *why have you put me here? Why? How can you just not care?*

The next day, just before noon, Little Eagle and Yellow Moon were resting on the beds in the lodge. The day was already hot and muggy. Running Otter interrupted their quiet when he returned to the lodge with a guest. It was Summer Breeze.

"This is Summer Breeze," he said to Little Eagle. Summer Breeze smiled her sweetest smile with her most innocent expression, but it still did not hide the evil that lived inside of her.

"How nice to meet you," she spoke, as she smiled her sweetest smile. Little Eagle shot a glare of contempt at Running Otter who seemed shocked by her reaction. Without thinking, Little Eagle turned toward Yellow Moon and rolled her eyes. Yellow Moon was able to stop the giggle that tried to escape her lips, but was not as successful at hiding the twinkle in her eyes. Little Eagle made a mental note that she needed to find out what Yellow Moon thought of Summer Breeze before she did or said something that might offend Yellow Moon. She did not want to offend the one person who seemed to be her one true friend.

The four of them sat around the lifeless fire pit, giving the appearance of a family. Yellow Moon had managed a few conversation niceties between herself, Running Otter, and Summer Breeze, but Little Eagle remained quiet.

After a few minutes, Running Otter addressed Little Eagle. "You should talk, too. You should get to know Summer Breeze."

Little Eagle raised an eyebrow and gave Running Otter a look that he knew all too well. He had seen it many times on the way back to the village. He now wished he had not prodded her to speak. Little Eagle spread a smile across her face that went ear to ear and turned her attention on Summer Breeze. "I understand that after the fall celebration that," she said, pointing to Running Otter's bed, "will be your side of the fire pit."

Summer Breeze was taken aback by the sudden and direct approach. She was always on the giving end of this tactic; never the receiver. "Yes, this is true. That will be my side," she smiled as she staked her claim.

"Good," Little Eagle answered. "I like it just fine over here," she said patting her own bedding. Running Otter's face wore a shocked expression. "It is only right that Running Otter's true wife be on that side of the fire," she said with mocked honor. As she continued speaking, she could not take her gaze off from Running Otter's expression. He had stripped her of her family, pride, and integrity and it felt good to see the favor returned. The fact she could do so made it even sweeter. She knew her behavior was not proper and never before had she ever spoken to or about someone with such disrespect, but she could not seem to stop. "Summer Breeze, darling, I'm sure you wouldn't mind taking him out behind the lodges so he'll stay over there now, would you?" she said still smiling sweetly. "Now, if you will excuse me I must go relieve myself." With that she stood up and left the lodge in stunned silence.

She really did not have to relieve herself. She had had her fill of playing family. Running Otter, Summer Breeze, and Yellow Moon would be a family, but she could not see herself being part of their family now. When Little Eagle began to replay what had been said at the lodge, she was a little afraid of what Running Otter might do to her for her behavior. After the shock wore off he was sure to be angry. Little Eagle was also aware that Yellow Moon did not follow her out of the lodge. This was the first time she had been alone since she was taken to Yellow Moon. She found it to be both refreshing and unsettling. Little Eagle made her way through the village and to the moss-covered earth beneath the trees where Yellow Moon took her in the beginning.

Little Eagle lay down on the moss and stretched out with arms folded under her head for a pillow. Quiet. She had longed for such a place. Little Eagle tried to piece together why she had reacted the way she did. As she lay there, she realized just how exhausted she felt and began to drift away with sleep.

Back at the lodge, Running Otter sent Summer Breeze home and sat staring at the empty fire pit. "I do not understand," he said to his mother. "I understood Summer Breeze's anger when I first took Little Eagle to my lodge. There is not love between Little Eagle and myself. Why is she reacting as if there is? I do not understand," he stated.

Yellow Moon remained silent for a few moments as she chose her words carefully. "You claimed Little Eagle as your wife only because you wished to save her from slavery, but then you told her you expected her to behave as your wife. She did as you asked." Anger began to rise in her voice as she spoke. "Now, before two full moons have passed, you are discarding her for another woman. She feels used and thrown away as if she were a slave being used and tossed aside. There is no difference! You saved her from nothing. This is why I asked you to wait until spring or next fall to take Summer Breeze as your wife." This was only one of the reasons, but she did not dare tell him she thought Summer Breeze was wicked and had hoped he would find love with Little Eagle and forget about marrying Summer Breeze.

Running Otter's anger subsided, "I cannot be angry with her for what is my fault," he sighed.

"Not even for saying she was sure Summer Breeze would be willing to go behind the lodges with you before you marry?" she asked while stifling a smile.

Running Otter gave a quiet snort, "No, not even for that. Truth is that ever since Summer Breeze got over being mad at me for taking Little Eagle to my lodge she has made more than one attempt to get me behind the lodges."

"What are you going to do?" his mother asked.

"I don't know," he said, leaving the lodge.

Little Eagle slept peacefully on the bed of moss until a fly began crawling first across her face, then her arm, only to return to her face and try to go into her nose. Little Eagle huffed and swatted at the pest repeatedly. She finally gave in and sat up while opening her eyes. She jumped with fright when she realized Running Otter was sitting on the moss next to her.

The man sat quietly staring into the woods. After a few minutes he spoke, "You were sleeping well," he started. "I did not mean to make you feel as you do. I thought you would be happy if I left you alone. I can wait to marry her if you want," he offered.

"But in the end you will still marry her?" she asked.

"I will," he answered.

"Then there is no reason to wait. Waiting will change nothing. You should marry the woman you want and not be stuck with a woman you only feel pity for," she said with an uncaring tone.

"I did not take you from the post because of pity. I took you because of respect," he told Little Eagle. "The marriage was already set before you came here."

"Yes, so you told me. I don't know what came over me that I spoke to you both that way. It was rude and unacceptable and I am sorry for my behavior. I don't know what happened," she mumbled.

Running Otter sighed and lay back on the moss. He had spent many summer afternoons lying here, resting and napping in the shade of these trees. This was a favorite spot for both he and his mother.

"I'm going to the stream for a drink," Little Eagle said as she rose to go, but dropped back to the ground. Running Otter was on his knees at her side in an instant, staring at her with concern. "I'm fine. I just stood up too quickly," she assured him. He helped her to her feet and walked her to the stream and waited for her to drink. When she stood back up he steadied her with a hand on her arm.

"I'm fine now," she said, pulling away from his grasp. He let her go, but walked closely as they returned to the lodge.

Running Otter walked her to her bedside and waited for her to sit, "she is not feeling well," he told his mother, "Keep an eye on her. She nearly fainted when she stood a while ago."

Yellow Moon eyed her with concern, but Little Eagle waved her away.

"I am fine," she repeated. "I stood up too quickly is all," she explained. Yellow Moon raised an eyebrow but said nothing.

Chapter 8

LITTLE EAGLE HAD more spells of light headedness the next couple of weeks. And she noticed that Yellow Moon had been trying to stuff her full of meats and green vegetables which added to the queasiness she was already suffering. One morning Yellow Moon asked her straight forward, "Are you with child?"

Little Eagle stared momentarily at Yellow Moon, "I believe I am," she answered. Yellow Moon smiled.

"I will make you tea that will help," she said, patting Little Eagle's arm. "You need to eat food that will help the baby be strong and to keep you strong. Have you told Running Otter?"

"No, I have not," she said dryly.

"Why?" Yellow Moon asked.

"In a few days he will take Summer Breeze as his real wife and he will be too busy to care about what happens with me," she snapped.

Yellow Moon gasped, "This is not true! You are his real wife just as Summer Breeze will be. This is his child. His first child. He will be very happy."

"Well, for now I will let his new wife be the center of attention. If Running Otter will be happy with her as his wife, I do not wish to do anything that would hinder their happiness," Little Eagle made an excuse. Truth was, the sting of rejection she felt from Running Otter still burned deep within her. The anger it caused made her feel selfish and without concern for anything that pertained to what would make Running Otter feel good about anything. *Eye for an eye,* she thought. She would keep this baby her secret for as long as she could. "I will tell him soon, but I really do not want to take away from their wedding." She lied, "The baby won't be here for many months so there is no reason to rush," she said, trying to ensure that Yellow Moon would keep her secret.

Yellow Moon stood silent for a few minutes then said, "I know what my son is doing has hurt you. The choice is yours. I will not tell." Yellow Moon hesitated, "don't close your heart to my son yet. You may find that over time closeness could be found with him that might become love."

Little Eagle raised her hand to object to any notion of her getting close enough to Running Otter to ever say that she had even the slightest feelings of love for him, but Yellow Moon raised her own hand to stop her from speaking.

"I did not come to Running Otter's father because we found love," she began, "I was from one of the sister villages of our people and had found love with a young handsome man who had proven himself in battle. He was strong and firm, but tender and gentle when he needed to be." she said with a fond remembrance. "We were to be wed soon, but my father, who was none of those things, saw a horse that he liked more than me and traded me to Running Otter's father. At first, I too, did what I had to do. He was a good man. Kind, gentle, and caring, but I kept a wall between him and me. About a year after Running Otter was born, the three of us were playing beneath the trees on the moss. As I watched the two of them play I realized that I had fallen in love with him."

Little Eagle was stunned and she knew at this moment she would be hard pressed to get anything over on this woman. She stepped forward and hugged Yellow Moon. Yellow Moon responded likewise.

"My heart is filled with joy," Yellow Moon said. "I will rejoice in secret."

Little Eagle smiled at the woman, "thank you."

Little Eagle thought often about what Yellow Moon had told her. It gave her understanding of who Yellow Moon was and how she had been able to show Little Eagle the compassion she had shown. But try as she might, she could not see herself in love with Running Otter.

It was not within her being.

The fall festival arrived and Running Otter took Summer Breeze as his second wife. For the first week after their wedding, the newlyweds spent their *getting to know you* time in a small empty lodge at the edge of the village. Little Eagle was delighted with the arrangement. She would have been ecstatic if it was permanent. Summer Breeze had been making a spectacle of herself every time Running Otter would bring her to the lodge for family bonding. Any time he paid attention to Little Eagle, Summer Breeze would find some way to draw the attention back to her.

Little Eagle and Yellow Moon were sitting by the outside fire when Running Otter and Summer Breeze returned to the lodge. "All good things must come to an end," Little Eagle said in a low tone as they watched the happy couple approach. Yellow Moon dropped her head and giggled, but made no reply. The two women stayed by the fire. Neither of them was in any hurry to start the new family unit.

"This is not going to be easy," Yellow Moon said softy, "always keep an eye on her and never trust her, daughter, she has a black heart," she finished as she took Little Eagle's hand in hers.

Little Eagle was caught off guard for two reasons. First, Yellow Moon had never said anything negative about anyone and second, she called her daughter. She swallowed hard as tears filled her eyes and felt the bond with Yellow Moon set as though it were stone. Little Eagle could not find the words to express her emotions. She accepted her place as Yellow Moon's daughter by squeezing her hand. Yellow Moon smiled and tightened her hold on Little Eagle's hand.

The day grew long as the two women sat by the fire, avoiding the inevitable. Finally, Yellow Moon sighed, "Come," she whispered, "we must feed the baby." The women giggled and rose from their seats. They were still smiling when they entered the lodge.

"Where have you been," Running Otter asked, not understanding why they had not rushed in to greet their return.

"We were enjoying one of the last good days before winter. It was hard to let it go," Yellow Moon answered.

Wow, how tongue-in-cheek was that? Little Eagle thought. It sounded like she was talking about the weather, but what she really meant was life before Summer Breeze. She turned away and busied herself with nothing to hide the grin on her face.

Summer Breeze sat perched beside Running Otter like an overly devoted wife eager to do his bidding. *The jobs all yours,* Little Eagle thought. Summer

Breeze said very little, but she smiled as though she was absolutely thrilled that they could all be a family. And Running Otter drank it up like fine wine. It was all Little Eagle could do to keep from rolling her eyes at the two of them.

Little Eagle's breath caught as a picture from her past flashed in her mind. It was the image of her and Robert after they had married. She – the overly devoted wife - and Robert, drunk on love. Pain, anger, and heartbreak rushed through Little Eagle like a tornado ripping, tearing, and pulling at every part of her emotions. She lay back on her bedding and rolled toward the wall, facing away from the others in the room.

Yellow Moon had seen Little Eagle's reaction and the gauntlet of emotions that ran through the young woman. She did not know what caused it and wished to comfort her, but she stayed put. Doing so would have drawn unwanted attention to Little Eagle. She understood that right now Little Eagle just wanted to be invisible.

When morning came, the foursome had breakfast in the lodge. The days were now chilly and the heat from the fires would be appreciated indoors. Summer Breeze was still smiling sweetly at everyone and playing the submissive newcomer. Little Eagle was just thinking that if it stayed like this, she would not mind the arrangement when Running Otter announced he was going out for a while. Summer Breeze smiled, held his hand briefly, and told him she would miss him. He smiled back at her, thrilled with attention that made him feel special. And then he left the lodge.

Summer Breeze stood quietly, waiting for Running Otter to get far enough away that he could not hear. She turned toward Yellow Moon, "You, go clean the dishes," then turning to Little Eagle she said, "You need to go gather firewood."

Both women stared at her for a few moments then stood up and left the lodge. "I was getting ready to clean the dishes," Yellow Moon said.

'Yes, I was going to help you and then get firewood, too." Little Eagle responded. "Looks like she wants to make sure we know who is in charge."

Yellow Moon nodded, "We will pay dearly for this."

"We would have paid dearly in the long run if we had obeyed like slaves," Little Eagle said. Yellow Moon nodded in agreement.

The two women went to visit Dragonfly for about an hour and then returned to the lodge. The dishes had been washed and firewood gathered and the lodge was empty when they arrived, but Summer Breeze must have been waiting for their return, because she came through the door right behind them and her eyes flashed with anger.

Summer Breeze stepped close to Yellow Moon's face. "There are things in this lodge that need to be done and I aim to see that they get done," she hissed.

Little Eagle pushed Yellow Moon aside before she could respond and then stepped between the two women. She stood inches from Summer Breeze's face. "This lodge ran just fine before you came. We don't need you to tell us what to do," Little Eagle countered.

"Don't mess with me or you will be sorry," Summer Breeze seethed with anger. A sound came from outside the door and Summer Breeze quickly stepped away.

Running Otter entered the lodge with a smile and sat down. Summer Breeze slid down beside him and began fondling. "It took most of the morning to get the dishes cleaned and the firewood gathered," she tattled. Running Otter looked from Yellow Moon to Little Eagle with a questioning expression.

"Oh, I must have misunderstood. I thought she wanted to do it by herself to impress you, it being her first day in the lodge," Little Eagle said ever so innocently. Running Otter turned toward his mother. She raised her brow and shrugged as if to say, "yeah, me too."

Little Eagle said, "We will make sure that we take care of the dishes and firewood tomorrow." Yellow Moon concurred with the nod of her head and smiled.

Summer Breeze's face still held an angelic smile, but her eyes were full of revenge.

That night Little Eagle wanted to scream. It started with Summer Breeze laughing just a little too loud, followed by moans that were borderline put on and then back to the giggling. Little Eagle prayed with all her might that Running Otter would tell her to be quiet and go to sleep. He never did, but she giggled herself, when in the midst of Summer Breeze's giggling, Running Otter started snoring. After that, the lodge was still with the exception of Running Otter's occasional snore.

The next day seemed to pass without much drama from Summer Breeze. The most she did was send a scathing glare at Little Eagle, but then Running Otter was there at the lodge for the greater part of the day.

Later that night, Little Eagle went out to relieve herself before going to bed. When she returned, the rest of them were already snuggled into their beds. As she slid into her bed, she realized it was full of small twigs, leaves, and dirt. She stood up and glanced at Summer Breeze, who was looking back with a smirk spread across her face. Little Eagle stooped and grabbed the buffalo hide by the edge and gave it a whip and a flip dislodging the items and causing them to spray across the fire pit and land on Running Otter and Summer Breeze.

"Oh, sorry, I had something in my bed," she feigned her regret. "Romp and giggle in that," she said to herself as she crawled into her clean bed.

On the other side of the fire pit, Summer Breeze was clearing their bed. Little Eagle rolled toward the wall and went to sleep with a smile on her face.

As the days turned to weeks, Summer Breeze had been a little more docile. The tricks that she pulled so far had back fired on her. Little Eagle was not sure if she had decided to keep her evil to herself or was trying to craft something that would not have repercussions. She did not really think the calm would last much longer. Running Otter was trying to bring Little Eagle into conversations and anything else he could. He was trying very hard to make this a real family without one wife more so than the other. He just could not seem to understand that he was the only one here that wanted this. Yellow Moon wanted Summer Breeze gone, Summer Breeze wanted Little Eagle gone, and Little Eagle just wanted to be left alone.

The calm before the storm ended by Running Otter kicking the proverbial hornet's nest when he asked Little Eagle to walk with him. Summer Breeze was on her feet and ready to tag along and make this as much about her as possible. Running Otter gave it a second kick when he said, "No, you stay today."

They walked to the mossy place beneath the trees and sat down. Little Eagle sat quietly for a few minutes then asked, "Do we need to talk?"

"No. I wanted to spend time with you without her vying for my attention," he said.

Little Eagle looked at him with surprise. "Yes, I noticed," he rolled his eyes. "I want her to learn that I will not hold one of my wives above the other," he finished. "Are you feeling better?" he asked with honest concern.

"Yes, Yellow Moon seems to know what to do about such things," she said, feeling a little guilty about the secret she was keeping.

Running Otter nodded, "good," he said as he stretched out on the moss.

Little Eagle was not sure what to think or feel about the attention she was getting. At first, she was not in favor of his attention, but then the more she thought about it, the more she realized it would get under Summer Breeze's skin like a chigger. She smiled and stretched out on the moss. She knew that taking pleasure in someone's suffering was wrong, but she justified it with her belief that God had forgotten her and such things did not matter here. Little Eagle's thoughts began to drift and she fell asleep.

"Little Eagle," Running Otter gently shook her from her sleep. "You should not sleep all day," he grinned. "We should go back now."

Summer Breeze had pouted the rest of the evening, but was once again trying to ensure that Running Otter stayed in her bed that night. It made Little Eagle smile to think that Summer Breeze was most likely almost crazy with jealousy over this afternoon; especially since all they did was talk briefly and then she fell asleep.

Little Eagle had slept late and rose in a hurry. She was in need of relief. It seemed she spent most of her time relieving herself or napping. She was lacing up her second moccasin when she realized something was wrong. Little Eagle removed the shoe to find that the bottom had been slit from toe to heel. "You," she yelled and was on her feet and closing the short distance between her and Summer Breeze. She stopped in front of Summer Breeze, "This is the second time you have done this," she said still clutching the moccasin. Summer Breeze gave her a twisted smile.

Running Otter entered the lodge just in time to see Little Eagle slap Summer Breeze across the face with the ruined moccasin. Summer Breeze stumbled then regained her balance and lunged at Little Eagle. Summer Breeze was stopped short by Running Otter.

"What is going on," he asked?

"This!" Little Eagle said as she shoved the moccasin at him. "This is not the first time she has done this, either."

"How do you know it was her?" he asked

"Did you do it?" Little Eagle questioned.

"No!" he responded with indignation.

"Well, I am sure Yellow Moon did not do it and I know I didn't do it. That leaves her," she said emphatically. Running Otter turned to ask Summer Breeze if she had anything to do with the ruined Moccasins, but frowned and hung his head when he saw the triumphant smile on Summer Breeze's lips. She had been so busy gloating over his shoulder she did not notice he was turning to face her. "You said this was not the first time."

"Remember when your mother was teaching me to make moccasins beneath the trees?" she asked. He nodded for her to go on. "We left our belongings there and walked along the river. When we returned both of my moccasins were cut just like this," she said, indicating the one she held.

Running Otter turned to Summer Breeze, "I thought I married a woman, not a child. Now take off your moccasins and give them to Little Eagle, then go to your mother's house and stay there until I come for you," he demanded. Summer Breeze's face was pale and she started to protest, but Running Otter pointed to the door and repeated, "Go!" Summer Breeze did as she was instructed and left the lodge at a near run. Running Otter sighed and shook his head. He stood for a few minutes as if he was not sure what to do and he left without saying a word. By this time Little Eagle's need was so great she dropped the shoes and ran out of the lodge barefoot.

When she returned, Yellow Moon chuckled at her for running out the way she did. Little Eagle giggled back.

The two women sat in silence for a little while then Little Eagle remarked, "I don't understand. She ruined two pairs of my moccasins and he punishes her by sending her to her mommy."

Yellow Moon looked stricken. "In our culture, for a man to say you are behaving like a child to his wife is a terrible thing, terrible," she repeated, "but for him to say 'you are a child. Go to your mother'...the only way it could be worse would be if he said to never come back."

"Worse for her, maybe, but best for us," Little Eagle commented without sympathy.

"Shhh," she cautioned as she smiled in agreement.

The two women went about their daily chores without stress or worry. That evening, Running Otter returned to the lodge alone. He sat by the fire and ate as though nothing was amiss. Little Eagle was expecting him to fetch Summer Breeze at any moment, but when bedtime came, he snuggled in his bed and fell asleep. Little Eagle figured he needed a night of not being mauled by Summer Breeze, whose motive was to ensure he stayed out of Little Eagle's bed. Summer Breeze was childish as Running Otter had said. An adult might have realized Little Eagle was not trying to compete for his attention or affection. All would be well if Summer Breeze would just stay over there and be his wife and leave Little Eagle out of the whole affair. As far as Little Eagle was concerned, it was a better situation than she could have ever hoped for. She had the position of a wife without wifely obligations. It was perfect. Running Otter had not come near her bed since he took Summer Breeze as his wife. If she could just get Summer Breeze to understand.

The following day was wonderful. Running Otter, Yellow Moon, and Little Eagle relaxed around the fire without Summer Breeze constantly drawing the center of attention back to her. Little Eagle thought Running Otter must have secretly felt the same way because he left Summer Breeze at her mother's for a second night. The next day, right before noon, Running Otter left the lodge and was gone for quite a while. When he returned, he had Summer Breeze in tow. Little Eagle frowned to herself but did take satisfaction from the fact that Summer Breeze was more than just a little rattled and unsure.

Running Otter instructed the barefoot Summer Breeze to make a pair of moccasins. She eagerly began her task to show what a good wife she was and because she had been looking forward to a new pair of moccasins. When Summer Breeze knew Running Otter was not looking, she flashed Little Eagle a smug grin of triumph. She may have taken a blow in the eyes of Running Otter, but she was going to get a new pair of shoes! Summer Breeze had been making moccasins since she was a child and made quick work of the task.

That evening, Little Eagle was awakened by a combination of Summer Breeze's irritating giggle and the need to relieve herself. She put on her moccasins and slipped out the door. The thought of having to go back inside and listen to Summer Breeze make a spectacle of herself made Little Eagle furious. How peaceful the nights without her had been.

When Little Eagle entered the lodge, she deliberately went to Running Otter's side of the fire, sat down and removed her shoes. Then feigning embarrassment, she turned toward Summer Breeze and said in a hushed tone, "Oh, sorry, I forgot." Little Eagle picked up her moccasins and went to the other side of the fire pit and crawled into her own bed. Her actions had the effect she had hoped for. Summer Breeze now thought Little Eagle had shared Running Otter's bed while she had been sent away and she now lay beside of him, pouting quietly. Truth was, he never asked and Little Eagle never offered.

The next day, as Summer Breeze was finishing the last shoe, she announced to Running Otter that she thought she would embellish the moccasins with some beading. Running Otter nodded in agreement that it would be a nice addition. She was thrilled with the knowledge that Running Otter thought it was a good idea. She spent the rest of the day smiling and beading. Now she would outshine Little Eagle, who now wore Summer Breeze's old moccasins.

That evening, she proudly presented her new shoes to Running Otter, who seemed to be very impressed with her speed and workmanship. She had recovered nicely from the ugly incident a couple of days ago and had stepped back into Running Otter's graces without a hitch. Summer Breeze's gloating came to a sudden halt when Running Otter took the moccasins from her hands and handed them to Little Eagle and told her to return Summer Breeze's shoes.

Little Eagle bit her bottom lip to keep her smile hidden. She had not expected this from Running Otter. The expression on Summer Breeze's face was priceless. At first, she was flabbergasted, which turned into outright rage. She was trying hard to hide her fury. Summer Breeze knew she was still treading on thin ice and it probably would not take much for her to get sent back to her mother's. That was too embarrassing. The village did not know why she was sent home by her husband, but they knew she had been sent. A good wife was never sent home!

Running Otter turned to Summer Breeze and said, "Nothing better happen to these moccasins. This must stop."

Summer Breeze hung her head in mocked shame. *For now*, she thought to herself.

The weather began turning colder as they approached the winter months, driving the village members indoors. For Little Eagle and Yellow Moon, this meant they were forced to spend even more time with Summer Breeze. The only time she would leave the lodge was if she were sure that Running Otter would not return to the lodge while she was away.

One chilly afternoon, Yellow Moon was kneeling beside the fire pit taking inventory of the soft rabbit pelts she had in her possession. She had a grandbaby on the way and had nothing ready for the arrival. She still had a few moons to wait, but the excitement was impossible to push aside. Summer Breeze, not yet knowing the secret, stood and crossed the lodge to where Yellow Moon sat and kicked the small bundle of furs before Yellow Moon into the corner.

"I will make any clothes Running Otter needs from now on," Summer Breeze said in a voice filled with a superior air.

Little Eagle started toward Summer Breeze, but Yellow Moon put her hand up for her to stop.

"Not everything that gets made in this lodge is for Running Otter," Yellow Moon's voice was hard and even as she stood up, "but if I wish to make something for my son, I will." Yellow Moon stood facing Summer Breeze with their gazes locked eye-to-eye. Little Eagle was not quite sure what to do or think. She had never seen this side of Yellow Moon and had always felt very protective of the seemingly defenseless woman. Yellow Moon had been passive about Summer Breeze up to this point, but it was now very clear that the one thing Yellow Moon would not allow was for Summer Breeze to push her around. Yellow Moon stood still as a rock and Summer Breeze tried, but she began nervously flexing her fingers.

"I would not mess with her, Summer Breeze," Little Eagle spoke.

"And why not?" Summer Breeze asked without moving her gaze.

"Because you are not a match for the both of us," Little Eagle said quietly.

A strange expression flashed across Summer Breeze's face. It was clear she had never thought about the fact that these two women could team up against her. She had assumed that Yellow Moon did not like the white woman and the white woman did not like Yellow Moon.

"You are right, Yellow Moon, not everything that gets made is for Running Otter," she stated as she made her retreat. Summer Breeze picked up her cape and left the lodge.

"I hope you tell Running Otter soon, Little Eagle, I cannot work on things for the little one without them knowing and asking questions." Yellow Moon said, "If you do not soon your belly will tell on you. When your dress pulls across your stomach just so, anyone can tell that you are with child," she finished.

"I will," Little Eagle sighed, "I just dread the misery that may come when she finds out."

Yellow Moon nodded in agreement, "We will face it together," she smiled as she retrieved her furs from the corner.

Running Otter pulled the buckskin door aside and stepped through the lodge door and dropped the hide door back in place. He stopped inside the door and began pulling his heavy cape over his head for removal. Summer Breeze must have been watching for his return, because she burst through the hide door behind him and ran right into his backside and sent him sprawling across the lodge with his cape still around his shoulders and head. He landed hard, narrowly missing the fire pit with his body, but the edge of his cape landed in the fire. Yellow Moon and Little Eagle sprang into action at the same time. Yellow Moon pulled the cape off from his head, freeing him as Little Eagle pulled the edge of the cape from the fire and began stomping out the flames. The smell of burning hair filled the lodge as the stunned Running Otter put together what had just happened. Summer Breeze still stood at the door, stunned by the commotion she had unleashed. Running Otter righted himself and approached Summer Breeze.

"Do you have any idea of the devastation and danger you almost caused? If Mother and Little Eagle had not been here, I could have been seriously injured or worse and the fire could have spread from our lodge to the others in the long house. This long house could have caused other lodges in the village to catch fire. Half the village could have burned, leaving people without homes while winter is upon us. There is nothing going on in this lodge that you need to be in such a hurry to see. You will enter this lodge like an adult, not a child!" Running Otter's voice was loud with anger.

Little Eagle winced at the scolding. She almost felt sorry for the woman. Almost. She watched as Summer Breeze's mouth opened to reply, but Running Otter turned his back to her. This was Summer Breeze's cue to keep silent and, fearing being sent home again, she went to sit by the fire.

There were only so many times of being sent home for a new bride before it became permanent. For some men, it took several times, and for some, once was enough. It depended on the man's temperament and the reason for being sent. Yellow Moon had explained the custom to Little Eagle right after Summer Breeze had been sent home. Being sent home was considered a shame on the woman and her family. From what she understood, it was equal to a bridegroom posting a sign in the middle of town telling everyone that his wife was too child-ish to be a married woman. Little Eagle was horrified at the prospect of such an embarrassment. She had wondered what he would do if she had displeased him and Yellow Moon's explanation had made her a little uneasy. Since Little Eagle had no family here, she would be traded or sold. Little Eagle decided that only a fool would get on the wrong side of Running Otter and purposed in her mind to never be that fool. She must tell him about the baby soon or risk being that fool. Little Eagle wanted the telling to be between the two of them, but Summer Breeze was making this impossible.

Summer Breeze remained still for a while, too afraid to push her luck, but she soon started rubbing Running Otter's shoulders. Running Otter sighed and began to relax. His anger with her had passed. Summer Breeze moved in on Running Otter like a panther on prey. The evening was filled with her giggling, petting, and flashing Little Eagle looks of victory.

Every giggle and smug look irritated Little Eagle until she could not stand it anymore and she started to speak.

"Running Otter," she interrupted Summer Breeze's giggling, "I have some-thing that I had wished to tell you privately, but I can never get alone with you," she continued as Running Otter knowingly looked at Summer Breeze, "it con-cerns the whole family, but began in private and is your right to make public."

Good, she had Running Otter's full attention. "I am with child. You will be a father in early spring," she smiled.

Running Otter was on his feet and closing the gap between them in an instant, then dropping to his knees beside of her. He stared at Little Eagle as though he could hardly believe the good fortune before him. Running Otter gently ran his hand across her small, round stomach. A smile crossed his face as the reality took root. He was going to be a father!

"This is good," he said with a laugh and sat down next to Little Eagle.

Little Eagle nodded and smiled.

Summer Breeze sat stricken as if something more terrible than being sent to her mother's had just happened.

Yellow Moon sighed, "Finally."

Running Otter turned toward her and asked, "You knew? Of course you did," he laughed. Running Otter would occasionally put his hand on Little Eagle's stomach as if he were confirming this was not a dream throughout the rest of the evening. Each time a smile would cover his face. Little Eagle found his reaction to be reassuring. She had not thought about how he would react, but now she was feeling relieved. Summer Breeze sat alone on her and Running Otter's bed, scowling when he was not looking and smiling as though she were just as overjoyed as he was when he looked in her direction.

It was getting late and Little Eagle was growing tired. "I think I will go to bed now," she told Running Otter and went to lie down in her bed.

Running Otter slid down beside her and said, "I would like to lie beside you for a while." Little Eagle said nothing and turned to face the wall as she always did every night. Running Otter lay down behind her placing his arm on her side with his hand resting on her stomach.

Running Otter leaned close to Little Eagle's ear and said, "If you wish to speak to me privately say so. She can leave us alone for a private word." Little Eagle smiled to herself. Running Otter was not naive. He was well aware of the game Summer Breeze was playing.

And for the first time in this lodge, Summer Breeze would sleep alone.

Chapter 9

WHEN MORNING CAME, it found Running Otter still snuggled against Little Eagle. They had both slept well. Little Eagle had been relieved that the secret was out and Running Otter was able to get some sleep without being pursued by Summer Breeze. Summer Breeze, however, had slept very little and was in a foul humor. She picked at her breakfast and shortly thereafter she left the lodge without a word to anyone.

Running Otter sat by the fire, smiling contently as Little Eagle and Yellow Moon discussed the things they would need to make for the baby. Cold weather babies required more than a warm weather babies. Around noon, Yellow Moon and Little Eagle dressed to go out and gather firewood and water. Running Otter left to tell friends about his good news. Little Eagle caught sight of Running Otter walking through the village as she and Yellow Moon returned from getting the water. She smiled and was sure that if Indians knew what a peacock was they would have changed his name.

The wood and water were gathered and the two women returned to the lodge to relax. They had the lodge to themselves for the moment.

"Running Otter is very happy about the baby," Little Eagle said.

"Did you think he would not be?" Yellow Moon inquired.

"I wasn't sure, I guess," she admitted.

Yellow Moon looked at Little Eagle questioningly, "I have never known a man who was not happy about his first child."

Little Eagle thought for a few moments then said, "I guess I haven't either. I thought it might be different because it was me, not Summer Breeze."

"You have much to learn about my son," she told Little Eagle.

"Speaking of the Wicked Wind," Little Eagle said, "what do you suppose she is up to?"

Yellow Moon laughed, "Nothing good, I'm sure," she answered.

Running Otter returned to the lodge with a chunk of fresh venison. Yellow Moon smiled as she took the meat. It would be a welcome change from the dried meat that usually accompanied the meals. Little Eagle poured water in the iron kettle and hung it from the tripod over the fire while Yellow Moon cut the venison into smaller pieces. Earlier in the day, Little Eagle had placed dried corn in a pot of water to soak for hominy. She now set the pot on the edge of the fire pit, balanced between two stones. Yellow Moon placed the meat cubes in the pot and Running Otter put a couple lengths of wood on the fire. Then the trio sat quietly on their beds and enjoyed the warm glow from the flames.

The bliss did not last long, though. Summer Breeze appeared through the hide door and went to sit down beside Running Otter. She looked rested and in a better mood. Little Eagle figured she had gone to her mother's and slept for a while.

Summer Breeze smiled at Running Otter, "I have something," she said pulling her hand from under her cape, "my family is very excited about having another baby in the family." She held out her hand for all to see the tiny moccasins.

Little Eagle's insides cringed at the thought of the baby being in the hands of Summer Breeze or anyone in her family. Little Eagle was positive the sun would never rise on the day that she would allow this to happen. She struggled hard to force a pleasant expression on her face. Little Eagle was sure this was all an act put on for Running Otter's benefit. From the delight that was radiating from Running Otter, Little Eagle would have to say that Summer Breeze was quite the actress and she knew her audience well. The moccasins were very cute, making it possible for both Little Eagle and Yellow Moon to show honest delight. The joy and excitement of a baby was contagious. *Maybe, just maybe, it would be the key to making a peaceful family*, Little Eagle thought.

The next few days passed with a peaceful rest in the lodge. Summer Breeze would chatter almost nonstop about the coming baby and how she was sure that she too would soon be with child. How wonderful it would be to have two little ones in the lodge. Running Otter was pleased with her acceptance of Little Eagle's child without any more problems between the two women.

As the days turned to weeks, Summer Breeze had even started helping Little Eagle and Yellow Moon cook and gather wood.

"There is no sense in you doing so much lifting and bending when there are three of us," she said to Little Eagle one day. "We must take care of your child." Summer Breeze's voice was brimming with sincerity as she handed Little Eagle a bowl of stew. With Little Eagle's growing stomach came the awkwardness of movement. Summer Breeze had made it her mission to wait on Little Eagle, bringing her food, water, and anything else she thought Little Eagle might be in need of. She was behaving toward Little Eagle as a friend. Summer Breeze would join Yellow Moon and Little Eagle when they worked on making clothing or other items that would be needed for the baby. Little Eagle and Yellow Moon had been very cautious at first, but it had been several weeks and Summer Breeze showed no sign of malice toward either of them. It appeared that they were finally melding into a functional family unit.

Summer Breeze had taken Yellow Moon's place when it came to gathering wood. She had told Yellow Moon she had carried enough wood in her life time and she should stay by the fire. That it was even an honor to carry wood for the mother of her husband. Yellow Moon however, stayed behind, but she did not sit by the fire. She had too much spunk for sitting. She would usually have their next meal in the works and the lodge set in order by the time they finished carrying wood and water. Summer Breeze had begun talking, laughing, and joking as if they were always friends. Little Eagle was actually enjoying Summer Breeze's companionship.

"I'm very happy that we can be friends now," Little Eagle told her one day. "I wished for so long you would understand that I did not wish to interfere with your marriage to Running Otter and would stay out of the way."

"It is better this way," Summer Breeze smiled as she patted Little Eagle's arm. "We are family and this makes Running Otter happy."

Little Eagle smiled and nodded her agreement; "Do you think you are with child yet?"

"No," Summer Breeze answered sadly.

"Don't be sad, maybe you are not far enough along to know yet," she encouraged. Summer Breeze brightened with a smile. "Maybe we should make double of everything now because I might be too busy to be much help in a couple of months," she added.

"We could make a few things," Summer Breeze said, "but don't forget that my family will be eager to help out, too."

"I guess where I am alone here I forget that you have family to help," Little Eagle explained.

"I don't think Yellow Moon would see it that way," Summer Breeze remarked.

"No, she would not," Little Eagle confessed with shame. "She is like a mother to me. I was very young when my mother died."

A little while after they ate their noon meal, Little Eagle became violently ill with a bad headache, followed by vomiting and diarrhea. At the end of an hour Little Eagle lay on her bed, completely spent. Nothing else remained in her stomach, but the dry heaving continued.

Yellow Moon put her cheek to Little Eagle's forehead. "You don't seem to have a fever," she remarked.

"No, I just hurt and I am sick," she answered as tears trickled down her face.

"I will make tea to help," Yellow Moon spoke quietly.

Little Eagle drank her tea and began to drift into a restless sleep only to be awaken by the need to vomit. Little Eagle tried to get to her feet, but fell back on her bed. She finally rolled on her side and vomited the tea.

When she caught her breath, she said, "I am sorry. I'm too dizzy to stand."

Yellow Moon hushed her and began cleaning up the mess as Running Otter lifted Little Eagle back in position on her bed and placed the blanket over her.

Running Otter, Yellow Moon, and Summer Breeze sat in silence. The only sound in the lodge was that of Little Eagle's labored breathing and moaning. Running Otter was the first to break the silence.

"I am going to Red Hawk's lodge for a while," he told his mother.

His eyes were full of sadness his mother noted as she nodded and said, "It may be a while before this is over."

"Send for me if you need me," he said as he left the lodge.

"I'm going to my mother's. Send for me if you need me," Summer Breeze parroted and left the lodge. Yellow Moon sat beside Little Eagle, rocking back and forth praying with all her might that this would pass and all would be well again. Yellow Moon thought the village seemed to be in the grip of an eerie stillness.

Dragonfly called to Yellow Moon from behind the hide door and Yellow Moon bid her to come in. "Running Otter stopped by on his way to Red Hawk's and asked me to come," Dragonfly told Yellow Moon.

"I am glad he did," she told Dragonfly, "I don't know what to think. She became ill very suddenly. There is no fever. I tried to give her medicine, but she cannot keep it down. I wish I knew what to do," Yellow Moon said as she hung her head. Dragonfly sat down beside her friend and placed a hand on her arm.

"I will stay with you for a while," Dragonfly said softly.

Yellow Moon nodded, "thank you, my friend."

Running Otter returned a while later. "How is she?" he asked with concern.

"She is the same," Yellow Moon answered in hushed tones as Dragonfly shook her head in confirmation.

When night fell there was no improvement in Little Eagle's condition. As the evening grew late, Dragonfly spoke, "Yellow Moon, you need to rest. Lie down and I will sit with Little Eagle. I will wake you if I need you."

Summer Breeze quickly interjected, "Oh, thank you, Dragonfly, but I can sit with her and you can go back to your family."

Dragonfly lifted an eyebrow and started to reply, but Running Otter stopped her, "I think it would be best if Dragonfly was with her. She has more experience with sickness. You should rest now. Mother may need your help tomorrow." Summer Breeze frowned at Dragonfly, but remained silent and turned to go to her bed.

That night was full of restless sleep. Throughout the night, Yellow Moon and Running Otter would awake and rise upon an elbow to check on Little Eagle. Dragonfly would silently shake her head "no." When morning came, the only change was that Little Eagle had begun to mumble incoherently. Two more days passed before Little Eagle began to show a small amount of improvement.

The incoherency had passed and the vomiting and diarrhea had stopped. This was however a bittersweet improvement. Her eyes were dark and sunken from dehydration and she was now having contractions.

"The contractions could be from the dehydration," Yellow Moon told Running Otter and Dragonfly concurred. Dragonfly mixed honey and water for Little Eagle drink while Yellow Moon retrieved the corn she had placed in water the day before to soak for hominy. Now that the kernels were plump with water she would press the juice from them. The leftover juice would contain sugar from the corn and help give her energy.

Running Otter stood, "I will be back soon," he said as he took his bow and quiver down from the peg on which they hung.

Yellow Moon and Dragonfly gave Little Eagle small sips of their drinks intermittently, but the contractions continued. An hour later, Running Otter returned with fresh meat and placed it in the pot of boiling water that hung above the fire.

Dragonfly sent Running Otter to the shaman to get herbs that were often used to slow labor and sometimes it would even stop labor. This was their hope and prayer. The two women administered the medicinal tea and waited. The tea eased the contractions some, but they continued and after a while they became harder and longer.

Late into the evening, Yellow Moon lifted her gaze from the floor and rested it on her son's face. Running Otter locked his own sad gaze eye-to-eye with her. Neither spoke a word, but words were not necessary. They both knew this was not going to end well.

A weary sigh escaped Running Otter as he stood and started toward Little Eagle. He stopped and turned to Summer Breeze, "You should go to your mother's until this over," he said. Summer Breeze leaped to her feet and started to object, but Running Otter went back to her and explained, "I fear that if you stay and then conceive that this could give you undo worry throughout your time." Running Otter brushed her cheek with his hand. "Please, so I will not worry for you," he finished softly.

"For you," she said and left the lodge.

After Summer Breeze left the lodge Running Otter went to Little Eagle's side. She stirred and opened her eyes. When she saw Running Otter she asked, "What is wrong?"

"I don't know. We have done everything we know to do and nothing helps."

Tears filled her eyes and ran across the bridge of her nose. "My baby," was the only words she uttered before the sobs racked her body. Running Otter lay down beside Little Eagle and held her in his arms and for the first time since his father's death many years ago, he cried. Yellow Moon and Dragonfly quietly slipped out of the lodge. They only stepped outside the hide door to give them privacy, but not so far that they could not hear Running Otter if he called for them. Both women leaned against the wall and quietly wept.

When the early morning light stretched across the sky, the air was rent with Yellow Moon and Dragonfly's death wail. Yellow Moon carefully laid the lifeless infant in a soft doeskin blanket and then placed a pair of tiny moccasins on his chest. Custom called for all Indians to be buried with a pair of moccasins so they would not be barefoot in the great hunting grounds in the afterlife. Dragonfly gently wrapped the doeskin around him snuggly and then she handed the baby to Yellow Moon who took the bundle outside the lodge. Running Otter and Red Hawk were waiting there to take the baby to be buried.

When Yellow Moon returned to the lodge Dragonfly had already given Little Eagle medicine to ease her discomfort from the delivery and to help her sleep.

"I made the medicine strong," Dragonfly told her.

"Good, she needs to rest," Yellow Moon agreed.

Chapter 10

DURING THE FOLLOWING weeks, Little Eagle regained her strength and returned to her daily routine. Her body was healing well, but her emotions were still shredded. She had given up hope that God even knew she still existed after her capture and now, with the loss of her child, she seemed unable to press forward. Summer Breeze was adding to the pain by constantly chattering about the baby she would soon be carrying. She would make comments about how she would make Running Otter happy when she gave him his first child.

Little Eagle became withdrawn and depressed. She went through the motions of life without any awareness of her surroundings. Yellow Moon tried repeatedly to draw her back, but to no avail. When Little Eagle did think about what had happened to her since that morning in the meadow, she only found questions without answers. How could God do this to her? Why had He let these things happen to her? She was taught and believed that she was loved by Him. He had shown her his love many, many times in the past. Had that changed? Her heart longed to cry out to Him for hope and healing, but her mind reasoned against her. Why had God dismissed Little Eagle? Night after night Little Eagle would go to her bed as tears filled her eyes and traced the bridge of her nose and she would silently ask, *"Why have you forgotten me, God?"* Sometimes this would be followed by quiet sobs, but most nights she was too tired and void of emotions to respond.

Spring was in full swing now and the flowers were in bloom everywhere. Little Eagle still asked the same question every night. She had healed emotionally a small amount, but mostly she had learned to hide the pain in her heart.

On the outside, she appeared to be fine; on the inside was a different story. She seldom left the lodge even though the weather was beautiful.

"Come with me," Running Otter told her one day.

Little Eagle followed him to the edge of the village before she asked, "Where are we going?"

"We are going for a walk," he said.

"Why?" she asked.

"Why not?" he responded.

Little Eagle shrugged her shoulders and shook her head. Running Otter stepped back to walk beside Little Eagle instead of in front of her.

"You need to get out more. The sun and fresh air will help the sadness go away," he began, "I have respected the fact that you would prefer to be left alone. I have been content with Summer Breeze in my bed, but I want you to know that if you find your heart wants another child tell me and I will come to you. I know your heart is still heavy," he said as he placed his arm around her shoulders while halting and turning her to face him. Little Eagle stared at his moccasins, unable to look him in the eye. Running Otter gently pulled her chin up to face him. "The decision will be yours, Little Eagle," he said softly.

Little Eagle managed a nod of understanding as tears filled her eyes and spilled down her face. Compassion squeezed Running Otter's heart as he saw deep into her heart. He instinctively pulled her close as she finally released the anguish she had been holding back. Running Otter held her until she quieted herself and then took her by the hand and began to walk again. They walked a few more yards when an eagle flew overhead and called out. Little Eagle looked to the heavens where the bird flew and once again tears filled her eyes and sobs shook her frame.

Running Otter waited for her to quiet herself again and then asked, "Why do you always respond to the eagle when he cries? That morning in the meadow, before we attacked, I watched you look up when he cried and many times since."

Little Eagle freed a weary sigh, "The eagle reminds me of my father, my home, and..." Little Eagle turned away. Running Otter nodded and lowered his head. He knew she was about to say her husband.

"There have been many times that I wished the war party had taken another path through the foothills," he confessed. "I wish you were with the man you loved, but I cannot undo that day. I did not want you to face the anger of the people in this village."

Little Eagle huffed in disgust, "I saw how tore up you were the day I ran the gauntlet. You were smiling and enjoying my pain and misery right along with everyone else!" she hissed.

Running Otter was slightly taken aback. "I was not laughing at you," he defended, "I saw the fire in your eyes when you dealt with Cold Water and I knew you could make it if you found that fire. The first time you ran it was not there, but the second time I saw the fire of determination flash in your eyes. That is why I smiled. I would never enjoy your pain."

"Oh," it was her turn to be taken aback. Little Eagle felt some of the anger she harbored against Running Otter fade. Yellow Moon had been right: she had a lot to learn about this man.

As the two stood, lost in their own thoughts, a rustling sound came from the bushes behind them. Running Otter and Little Eagle turned just in time to see Summer Breeze step out into the open.

"There you are. I come to tell you the food is ready," she explained.

"I am sure it is," Running Otter sighed as he and Little Eagle began walking toward the village.

Neither of them believed her concern was their hunger. She could not bear the thought of Running Otter showing Little Eagle any attention.

Summer Breeze quickly pushed between the two of them and began her usual chatter, "Won't it be wonderful when I have a child and we can take our son for walks with us?" she said with an innocent smile.

Running Otter stopped and said, "Little Eagle go on ahead. I would like to speak with Summer Breeze privately."

Summer Breeze beamed with delight as Little Eagle nodded her head and continued walking toward the village.

"Summer Breeze," Running Otter started to scold, but then thought better of it, "I would like for you to keep the talk of our future babies between us for a while."

"Why?" she pouted.

"I want it to be a special thing between just the two of us," he lied. The truth of it was that he could see how her constant chatter about babies was hurting Little Eagle and some days he had suspicions that she may have been doing it just for that purpose. Lodge life had been peaceful and he did not want to say anything that might disrupt the peace and cause Summer Breeze to behave as she had previously.

Summer Breeze on the other hand was eager to comply if it meant Running Otter thought this was something special between the two of them. She was willing to participate in anything that excluded Little Eagle.

Later that night, when Summer Breeze stepped out to relieve herself, Little Eagle told Running Otter, "Thank you for this afternoon."

"Things will get better with time," he promised. "Remember what I said about another child. The choice will be yours."

"I will remember, but I don't think I want to," she told him. Running Otter nodded.

Little Eagle felt weary and went to settle into her bed. Before she had distanced herself from God she would have called on Him to give her strength and comfort; to give her rest from the troubles and cares that she now carried. The only thing she had now was confusion and the feeling of being alone and tossed about. How could she find God again in this place? He seemed so far away.

"I don't know how to reach you," she whispered as she looked toward the heavens through the smoke hole in the roof. Tears slipped across her temples to wet her hair. "Find me, please," she continued as her body shook while trying to hold back the sobs. Little Eagle was unaware of Yellow Moon's presence until after Yellow Moon had lain down beside side her and was wrapping her arms around her. Little Eagle rolled toward Yellow Moon and sobbed against the woman's chest. After a while, Little Eagle began to quiet. It was then she realized that Yellow Moon had not just held her, she had cried with her. Little Eagle was in awe. Here in the middle of this unbelievable nightmare her Heavenly Father had given her a mother. Fresh tears filled her eyes.

"You are a good mother. I love you, Yellow Moon," she whispered to the woman.

Yellow Moon sniffed, "I love you, Little Eagle," and then she gave Little Eagle a squeeze.

Little Eagle snuggled against Yellow Moon and sighed. She was asleep in minutes.

A couple of weeks later, the camp filled with commotion one afternoon as Little Eagle and Summer Breeze were carrying water. The women took the water to the lodge where Yellow Moon as working on hides. Then the three women went to see the source of the disturbance. When they reached the area, many people had already gathered and it was impossible to figure out what was going on. There were so many people there you could not see anything and the noise from everyone made it impossible to hear. After a few minutes, the chief and elders of the village managed to get to the center of the throng. The trip back out of the crowd was quicker. Anyone who did not give way to the elders was given a good whack with the chief's walking stick. Right of way belonged to the leadership of the village. Indian culture demanded respect for those in charge. Disrespect would not be tolerated by anyone.

As the group of men passed by, Little Eagle could see the cause of the ruckus. The village was being visited by a missionary. He wore a black robe covered in dust and mud with a leather pouch hanging from one shoulder by a strap and a brown dusty coat slung over the other shoulder. As he walked passed Little Eagle, he turned his head and looked her directly in the eye and smiled. Little Eagle stared expressionless in return and then turned and walked away. *"What business did he have smiling at her like that?"* she asked herself.

The next few days Little Eagle managed to avoid him. She was uneasy about getting near this man. After all, she had been very angry with God. She had accused Him of not caring what happened to her and for putting her out here in this forsaken place. She was afraid of being punished for her ways. And then there was the fear that she might find out God really did not care and had forgotten her.

One evening, Running Otter came back to the lodge and sat down beside Little Eagle. "The holy man wants to talk to you," he told Little Eagle.

"Why?" she asked, her eyes wide with worry.

"I did not ask," he answered.

Little Eagle was silent for a few moments and then said, "I don't think I want to."

Running Otter raised his brows and asked, "Why?" Little Eagle just shrugged. Running Otter thought for a while and then said, "I think you should. Maybe he can help your heart heal. You can talk with him tomorrow afternoon," he continued.

Little Eagle knew from Running Otter's tone that the matter was already decided. She would be talking to the holy man.

"I will go for him after we eat and then we will go and let you speak with him here in…"

"No!" she interrupted. "I mean, I would rather meet with him along the river. That way no one will have to be troubled to leave," she explained.

The truth was that she wanted the option of escape. If she wanted or needed to end the visit she could just walk away, but here in the lodge it would be very rude for her to leave a guest sitting alone in her own home. Then there was the fact that Summer Breeze had been noticed hanging around the thin hide walls, trying to overhear things that were not her concern.

"You can meet with him by the river if you wish," he agreed with a questioning look.

"I can get more sun and fresh air that way," she smiled.

Running Otter nodded, but knew there was more to it than fresh air. She could meet the holy man in the middle of the river if she wanted, just as long as she met with him. He was at his wits' end. Ever since that fateful day in the meadow when he found her, he had hoped for the best for Little Eagle. He had made decisions that he thought were for her good, but he always seemed to cause more pain and disappointment for her. Little Eagle was on a downward spiral that frightened him. She had been so full of vitality in the beginning and now she seemed to barely exist from day to day. This holy man was his last hope. He had noticed that she would pray in the beginning and that had sustained her strength, both mentally and physically, but then the prayer stopped she began to withdraw into nonexistence.

This woman had affected him in ways he never thought another human being could. She had made him question himself as a warrior. Could he lead men in battle now and still be as detached from the enemy as he once was? Or would he cower at the weight of the responsibility that came with such decisions? Before she came here, the cost of his actions was left on the battlefield.

That night was a long night for both Running Otter and Little Eagle. Little Eagle worried that tomorrow's meeting would open old wounds that she wanted left alone and Running Otter feared that the holy man would not be able to return the spark of life that he cherished back to Little Eagle.

The sun slowly made its appearance and the village stirred itself awake. Little Eagle had been awake for a while, but stayed in her bed listening to the morning sounds. Seldom did the sounds of morning change. The birds were first to wake and sing. This was followed by the hushed female voices moving about as they prepared food. There would be an occasional male voice and a sporadic dog bark. Eventually, the sound of children would begin to fill the air and the volume would rise just a bit as the village reached full swing. Little Eagle listened until Yellow Moon awoke and then rose to help her begin the day's routine.

Little Eagle was making peace with the fact she was going to meet with the holy man. She would have to admit there was a stirring of excitement within her being. It was a mixture of emotions for her. Feelings of dread and fear of the unknown mingled with expectation and hope. When the time came for the meeting, Running Otter walked with Little Eagle toward the river. As they approached, she could see the holy man standing by the river, watching the river lazily flow south. He turned toward them when he saw their reflection in the water as they approached. He smiled and raised his hand in greeting. Running Otter took Little Eagle's hand and stopped short of their destination. Little Eagle turned to face him.

"Stay as long as you wish. There is no hurry," he spoke encouragingly.

Little Eagle gave no response as she turned and walked toward the waiting man. The holy man smiled and raised his hand in greeting to Running Otter. Running Otter waved a return greeting and then turned and walked away. Little Eagle stopped beside the holy man, not sure what she should do next.

"Hello," he spoke.

Little Eagle nodded, "Hello."

"Shall we walk?" he asked as he pointed downstream. Little Eagle remained silent, but began walking in the direction he had indicated.

"I am Father Humphrey," he introduced himself as he fell into step beside Little Eagle, "What is your name?"

"I am Little Eagle," she answered.

"This I already know. What is your Christian name?" he asked.

"I don't have one," she countered, "I am Little Eagle."

Father Humphrey sighed, "Who were you before you became Little Eagle?"

"That woman died in a meadow with her husband about a year ago," she said with indifference.

"Okay," Father Humphrey decided to go along with her insistence. "What was the dead woman's name?"

It was Little Eagle's turn to sigh, "Her name was Micah Phillips and her husband's name was Robert."

"Running Otter told me how you came to be here. That he found you in a meadow building a house. Where did you live before the meadow?" he prodded.

Little Eagle did not like the subject this man seemed to be consumed with. She had done everything possible to put that life behind her and tried to never think about it. "She," Little Eagle said, removing herself, "lived in another meadow near a place known as Blue Knob in the eastern foothills. I don't know where any of her family is now." she stated, hoping to stave off any more prying questions.

"Would you like to sit?" he asked.

"No," she answered. She was too nervous to sit still.

"You are treated well?" he asked.

"I have been treated well ever since the day Running Otter took me to his lodge. His mother is very dear and sees me as a daughter. Running Otter took a second wife. She has not always been nice to me, but she has been of late," she explained.

"Good, good," he nodded.

"Why are you here? What do you want?" Little Eagle blurted the questions.

"I am here to tell you that God has not forgotten you. He knows where you are and is just as willing to be there for you as he was before you ended up here. He loves you," Father Humphrey replied.

Little Eagle felt her heart squeeze as tears filled her eyes and she quickly wiped them away. "How can you say that? Look where I'm at! Even if I could leave here and return home I would be shunned by everyone because I have been the wife of an Indian!" She spit the words out like they were poison.

"You blame God for what has happened to you, do you not?" he asked.

"I do," she confessed.

"I don't know the answers to all of the questions that torment you, but I will tell what I do know. Our heavenly Father gives us free will, meaning we can do as we choose. We can serve Him or we cannot. Some of the things that befall us are because of the choices we make. When you and your husband started west, did you have any misgivings about the move?" he hesitated for a couple of seconds as if he did not expect an answer. "What I am saying is at times we make choices that are not in our best interest. Sometimes the consequences are small and insignificant and other times they may cost us everything, maybe even our lives. And at other times we do nothing wrong, but we get blindsided by the enemy. Scripture tells us that the devil goes to and fro searching for someone to destroy. Many times it is a combination of bad choices and the enemy working against us. We make decisions that are out of His will and protection, leaving us vulnerable to the attacks of the enemy. But no matter the reason for our situation, one thing is always true. God will always walk with us through everything. Whatever the reason, God will turn things around for our good if we trust Him," Father Humphrey was finally silent.

Little Eagle was a little upset at this point for a couple of reasons. He had indicated that she may bear some responsibility for her present situation and secondly, she knew there was truth to what he had said. She did have misgivings about the move, but she had brushed them aside to please Robert. She would not be here now if she would have spoken her heart. Little Eagle stopped walking and sat down on a large rock along the river's bank. She had been so angry with God, blaming him for everything she did not like about her life. She had been looking for ways to lay blame on God instead of looking for the things He was doing on her behalf. Tears slid down her face and landed on her dress.

Father Humphrey placed a hand beneath her chin and pulled it upwards to face him. "Put aside how or why you are here. You must see how God has covered you with His hand. Things were in motion for you to die that day in the meadow, but God gave you the words needed to spare your life. Your chance of survival after you were taken captive was still zero. After running the gauntlet, you were to die. Yet here you are. You were moments away from becoming a slave when God moved on Running Otter's heart to spare you yet again. There is not a better man in this village to have as a husband." Father Humphrey let go of her chin and turned to squat beside Little Eagle. "Please, understand just how much He loves you. I left my home six months ago at God's bidding. I have carried a purpose in my heart to find you and tell you that you are not forgotten. I have traveled hundreds of miles through almost as many villages looking for the one I was sent to find. I have ministered to several captives, but knew that I had not found the one I was sent to find until I saw your face in the crowd the day I arrived. When I leave here, I will be returning to my family. I have completed what God had asked of me."

The two of them sat silently for a few moments. Then Father Humphrey stood up.

"I think we have talked enough today. I will leave you with your thoughts." Before turning to leave, Father Humphrey placed his hand on Little Eagle's shoulder. She felt the warmth of God's love flow over and through her. Tears began to well in her eyes as she struggled to control the sobs that were trying to erupt. Father Humphrey removed his hand and walked away, but the warm and loving hand of God remained. Little Eagle submitted herself to the love that knows no bounds. She cried, letting the tears cleanse her of anger and pain. When her tears stopped, she felt new and content. Her heart had longed for the presence of God and now she was satisfied. Little Eagle knew she could now face tomorrow and put the past behind her. When she thought about the child she lost, she still felt loss, but now there was hope.

Little Eagle went to the river bank and carefully made her way down the bank side and out onto a sandbar. She knelt down at the water's edge and washed her face. The cool water was refreshing. Little Eagle then drank her fill of water.

"Now what?" she asked, looking toward heaven. Little Eagle made her way back up the river bank and started toward the village. She had been afraid of the holy man. Now she wondered why she had feared him. He only had good things for her. She was still trying to wrap her mind around the fact that God had sent this man traipsing across the countryside in search of her. God and father Humphrey cared that much!

When Little Eagle returned to the lodge, Running Otter asked, "Did the talk go well?"

Little Eagle thought for a moment. She had said very little during the visit, "It went well," she nodded. It was still early in the evening, but Little Eagle was exhausted. She was at peace and felt like she could really sleep for a change. Little Eagle slid beneath the cover and drifted into a restful sleep.

Chapter 11

LITTLE EAGLE AWOKE to the sound of the village as it began to stir. She smiled as she remembered her visit with Father Humphrey the day before. The others in the lodge were still sleeping when she slipped out into the morning air. There was something refreshing about the smell of the morning air. Little Eagle had a purpose in mind this morning. She wanted to be away from the others so she could bare her heart to the Lord. Little Eagle made her way to her favorite spot beneath the trees. There she knelt down on the moss and began to pray for the first time in several months. *"Lord,"* she began, *"I have been blaming You for the things that have happened to me. Please forgive me. I am partly to blame. I have been holding feelings in my heart that are not good. I wish to lay them down now and I ask You to help me do so. I wish to let go of anger, bitterness, blame, and un-forgiveness against myself and …"* tears and emotions overwhelmed Little Eagle as she stretched out, face-down on the moss covered ground. She had longed for her Heavenly Father's presence and now He was here. She had believed that He could not find her, or that He did not wish to, but she had been deceived. He knew where she was all the time. She only needed to call out to Him. Little Eagle cried as the perfect peace of God washed away her misery. When she had emptied herself of the things that vex her, Little Eagle rolled over onto her back and looked up at the sky. She had not seen a sky as blue as this one in a very long time. As a matter of fact, everything seemed more beautiful than it had for some time. She still wished that none of the things that had transpired over the last year had ever happened, but now from deep within she found hope. As Little Eagle lay upon the moss, reflecting on her new-found hope, an eagle soared overhead and rent the air with its cry. Fresh tears filled her eyes. She was awestruck. So many times in her life the eagle's cry had reminded her of the scripture her father had often quoted: *they that wait upon the Lord shall renew their strength*. The eagle's cry had always given her hope and brought back fond memories of her father. Even the Indians had given her the name Little Eagle. God had been with her always, but she had failed to see it. God's grace was truly amazing. She had become angry and turned away from Him, but He still stood by her, loving her no matter what. God loved her so much He sent Father Humphrey here to tell her just that.

Little Eagle rose and went to the river to wash the tears from her face. When she looked at the reflection in the water, she no longer saw a face without hope, but instead found the face of Micah Little Eagle. Little Eagle smiled and began making her way back to the lodge, gathering wood as she went.

When she arrived back at the lodge, the others were up and had already eaten. Running Otter and Yellow Moon smiled when they saw the peaceful expression on her face. Summer Breeze stared at Little Eagle like a caged animal wanting to get away. Yellow Moon handed Little Eagle a bowl of food as Summer Breeze excused herself and went to her mother's.

"You are feeling better?" Running Otter dared.

"I am," she smiled.

"The holy man is good medicine," he said with a smile.

Little Eagle nodded, "I would like to see him again if it is alright."

"You may see him as much as you like," Running Otter said.

"Thank you," she said as she finished her breakfast. "I will go after I get water and firewood."

"Summer Breeze can get the water and firewood today. It has been a few days since she drew water or gathered wood," he stated.

Little Eagle raised her brow but said nothing. She had not been aware that he knew Summer Breeze would pick and choose when she helped with chores. Summer Breeze was all about helping when Running Otter was around to see her helping, but not so much when he was away.

Later that morning, Little Eagle spotted Father Humphrey sitting on the ground, reclining against a tree, watching a group of children playing. He smiled and waved when he spied Little Eagle approaching.

"Good morning," greeted Father Humphrey.

"Good morning," she smiled as she sat down beside him.

"How are you this fine morning?" Father Humphrey inquired.

"I am very well and I have you to thank for that. So, thank you," she said with gratitude.

"I would do it all over again, my dear," he smiled as he patted her arm. "I will be leaving soon. If I leave now I will be able to return home before winter."

"Do you have family?" Little Eagle asked.

"I do; A wife and two small boys. Well, they were small when I left them last fall," he answered.

"You must miss them very much," she commented, "Will you tell them I said thank you for allowing you to come here?"

Father Humphrey smiled and nodded. "Remember to love and honor God where ever you are and He will work all things out for your good."

"Have a safe journey home, Father Humphrey," Little Eagle said as she stood.

"Go with God, Little Eagle," he said as she walked away.

The next few weeks passed with the usual daily routine. The only difference was Little Eagle. She had made peace with her situation and had given thought to Running Otter's offer of another child. She had decided that she would approach the subject with Summer Breeze. Summer Breeze had been so excited about the two of them having children at the same time.

One afternoon, Yellow Moon was out visiting with Dragonfly and Running Otter had gone down river with some men earlier in the day. Little Eagle decided she would tell Summer Breeze about her desire to have another child.

"Do you think you are with child yet, Summer Breeze?" she began.

"Not yet," she stated, "but soon, I think."

"I think I am ready to try again," Little Eagle admitted.

"Try to what?" Summer Breeze questioned.

"To have a child," Little Eagle answered.

"A child!" Summer Breeze roared, "I just got rid of the last one!"

"What?" Little Eagle asked shocked. "What do you mean got rid of?"

Summer Breeze realized she had let the cat out of the bag, but recovered and decided to plunge head long into the matter. She was so tired of playing nice with this woman.

"I mean exactly what I said," she hissed. "I thought the poison would never work. I was beginning to think that I was going to have to smother that little rat while you slept!"

"You poisoned me?" Little Eagle said, dazed and trying to comprehend what had been said.

"Yes, and you will never give birth to Running Otter's child. I will not allow it! I only wish you would have died, too."

The truth of Summer Breeze's words finally hit home with Little Eagle. Summer Breeze had killed her child! Little Eagle stared in disbelief at Summer Breese for a fraction of a second and then leaped at Summer Breeze. Little Eagle clasped her hands around her throat as her anger burned out of control. Summer Breeze punched Little Eagle in the stomach hard, causing her to lose her grip on her throat. Summer Breeze pushed Little Eagle away, causing her to sprawl on her backside. It was then that both women realized Running Otter was standing inside the doorway.

"Running Otter," Summer Breeze called, "Little Eagle has lost her mind. She attacked me for no reason!"

"No reason!" Little Eagle screamed.

Running Otter threw his hand up and shouted, "Silent!" his face was dark with anger as he crossed the room and grabbed Summer Breeze by the arm.

"Running Otter she…" Summer Breeze began.

"Silent!" he said as anger consumed his words. "I heard enough."

Summer Breeze's face was horror-stricken as Running Otter pulled her from the lodge.

Little Eagle had stood to her feet as soon as Summer Breeze pushed her away. She now stood alone in the lodge stunned, trying to absorb what she had just learned.

She was still standing there when Yellow Moon ran through the doorway.

"What has happened?" she asked as she went to Little Eagle. "Running Otter said you needed me."

Suddenly, Little Eagle felt faint. She half sat and half fell to the floor. Yellow Moon kept asking her if she was alright and what had happened, but she was still too shocked to form the words. As the shock wore off, she began sobbing uncontrollably. Moments later, Running Otter returned alone. Yellow Moon looked at him helplessly as she held the weeping woman.

"What has happened?" she asked.

Running Otter took a deep breath, "Summer Breeze gave Little Eagle poison and that is why she lost the child," he said as he took Little Eagle in his arms.

Yellow Moon stared at him in disbelief momentarily. "I will leave you for a moment," she said as tears began to streak her son's face.

"Mother, bring something back to help settle Little Eagle," he said as she slipped out the door.

Running Otter held Little Eagle and let her cry. There was nothing he could say that would make any difference.

A few minutes later, Yellow Moon returned with a cup of medicine. "I made it strong," she told him as her own tears fell to the lodge floor. Running Otter nodded as he took the cup and held it to Little Eagle's lips. She drank most of the tea. Running Otter drank the tea that remained. He moved Little Eagle to her bed and gently laid her down, then lay down beside her and wrapped his arms around her, pulling her close. Minutes later, the tea began to quiet Little Eagle. Eventually the medicine won and she slept. Running Otter could feel the tea taking affect. He willingly allowed the medicine to work. This was one nightmare he wished to escape, even for a little while.

When morning came, he still held Little Eagle in his arms. Her eyes were red and swollen. He had been awakened by her sobs as she cried in her sleep during the night. He knew she had taken the loss of the child hard, but he had not realized just how hard until now.

"Where is Summer Breeze?" Little Eagle asked.

"She is gone," he answered.

"What do you mean, gone?" she asked.

"She will not be returning."

"You returned her to her mother?"

"No," he replied. "I will not allow any woman who would harm my child to live in this village."

"You…killed her?" she asked shakily.

"No, she will be marked," he told her.

"What do you mean she will be marked?" Little Eagle asked.

"She will be given the mark of a murderer," he said without feeling. "I am sorry that I brought her into this lodge, Little Eagle."

"Looking back will only bring us sorrow," she said as she laid her hand on his arm. "We will only look forward to what the future may hold for us," she finished with a faint smile. "She has caused us to mourn for the last time."

Running Otter nodded in agreement, "her name will never be spoken in this lodge again. We need to go now."

"Go where?" she asked.

"It is time for the marking," he answered.

"I have to go?" she asked, "Can you go in my place or something?"

"All who are involved are expected to appear at the sentencing," he explained. "Come," he said as he motioned with his hand.

Little Eagle and Yellow Moon followed Running Otter out of the lodge and to the crowded council house. Summer Breeze stood in the center of the council house with her hands bound behind her. Summer Breeze's head hung forward with her hair hanging in a ratty mess that covered her face. A short distance from her burned a fire with a length of wood with one end lying in the flames.

Running Otter lead them to the center of the room and sat down in the front row. Running Otter and Yellow Moon seated Little Eagle protectively between them.

When Little Eagle looked at Summer Breeze, she still found her mind filled with disbelief. "*God give me grace*," she prayed. Little Eagle knew that she could never understand the senselessness of what Summer Breeze had done. She made a decision at that moment that she would do her best with God's help to forgive the things from the past, even the evil this woman was guilty of and put it behind her. For her to dwell on this, it would consume and destroy her and her future. Her Christian teaching had taught her that when we forgive others for the things they do to us it releases them into God's hands so that He can deal with them justly. To hold onto un-forgiveness puts limits on God. If we want to be forgiven for the things we do wrong, then we must forgive others.

Sitting in the front row, almost opposite of Little Eagle, sat Summer Breeze's family. Their faces where set like blank slates, but their eyes told the true story that hid behind the slate faces. Little Eagle's chest squeezed with compassion for them. She could not imagine the tormented thoughts they were feeling. Your own kin, whom you dearly loved, being guilty of such a crime. Little Eagle could not breathe and was on the verge of hyperventilating when both Running Otter and Yellow Moon instinctively grabbed hold of her hands. Neither one said a word as they both understood Little Eagle had never witnessed such a judgment being carried out. This was not the white man's law.

Yellow Moon could remember one other time in her life that she had witnessed judgment against someone for murder. It had been when she was younger. A man had beaten his wife to death. She found it haunting and confusing because men beating their wives was not uncommon among these people. It seemed to be alright for you to beat your wife as long as you did not kill her while doing so. At the request of the dead woman's father, the man who had transgressed had one hand dismembered so he could not beat anyone in this life or in the life to come. The man fainted and then ended up bleeding to death because no one would come to his aid after the sentence was carried out. The man had been her uncle. She had always believed this incident was the only reason her father had not beaten her mother to death. Yellow Moon placed her free arm around Little Eagle's shoulders. This would not be easy for Little Eagle. Yellow Moon knew this woman, like herself, did not enjoy the pain and misery of others.

The chief, Cold Water and several leaders from the village entered the meeting house and approached the center of the room where Summer Breeze stood. The men standing in the center of the room were the only ones who knew why they were there. Not even her family knew yet. They were only told that she was to stand before the council. Most of the people in attendance believed they were there to witness a divorce since she had a history of being sent home to her mother.

Running Otter turned to Little Eagle and when she turned and looked him in the eyes he could see the pain and uncertainty that raced through her mind, "This must be done. Our people are free to live as they choose and we have few laws, but the laws we have are to be followed for the penalty is harsh," with that said, he stood and faced the center of the room.

"Running Otter, tell all who are here why you have called for this meeting," Cold Water commanded.

"I Running Otter, wish to make it known that I am no longer married to this woman. She is unfit to be a wife or mother."

Summer Breeze's family hung their heads in shame as quiet gasps filled the room. Summer Breeze still stood with her head down as though she heard nothing around her.

Cold Water spoke again. "Have you anything else to say?"

"Yes. I heard this woman say that she poisoned my wife, Little Eagle, and our unborn child. Our child died because of this. She is guilty of murder. Any woman who would kill a child of mine…" his voice broke.

By this time, the council house was beginning to roar with the voices of shocked and exasperated people. Tears began to trace Little Eagle's face as she looked from Summer Breeze, who still made no response, to her heartbroken family. Summer Breeze's mother and sisters were being shaken by uncontrollable sobs. Her father held his wife, trying to sooth her as his own face glistened from tears.

Cold Water shouted for the room to be still and an instant hush filled the room. "What sentence are you asking to be carried out, death or marking by fire?" he asked.

"Marking by fire," he answered.

"Is there anything else you want to add to this?" he questioned.

"She is to be taken north and given to the traders who trade with our enemies. They will be told to trade her to our enemies, I will not tolerate her living in this village or any sister village." he said as the council house erupted again.

Cold Water nodded. "It will be as Running Otter has said," he shouted over the uproar. Then Cold Water stepped before Summer Breeze, wrapped his hand in her mangled mass of hair and pulled her head up to face him.

Summer Breeze managed to tilt her head toward Little Eagle. Her eyes locked on Little Eagle as a sinister smile flashed across her lips. Little Eagle saw the same dark, hating evil staring at her that had been there the first time she met Summer Breeze by the cooking fire. It was clear that there was no repentance in

Summer Breeze. She had hated Little Eagle so much that the fact the child she killed was also Running Otter's made no difference. Little Eagle wept openly.

Cold Water stretched forth his hand and one of the other men retrieved the length of wood from the fire and handed it to him. Cold Water looked toward Running Otter with a silent question passing between them. Running Otter held up his hand and shook his head "no". Cold Water turned back toward Summer Breeze and pressed the red hot coal against her left cheek. Summer Breeze screamed a horrifying sound and the room fell silent.

Little Eagle's stomach began to churn and her head felt light as the smell of burned flesh reached her.

Yellow Moon had been keeping an eye on Little Eagle and feared she could take no more, "Running Otter, please..." she called to her son.

Running Otter turned his attention to his mother and quickly realized Little Eagle had had enough. Yellow Moon and Running Otter helped Little Eagle to her feet and walked her out of the council house. The world whirled around Little Eagle as her legs failed to support her. Running Otter caught her in his arms and began to carry her toward their lodge. They had not gone far when she told Running Otter to put her down. Little Eagle vomited as soon as her feet were under her.

"Take her back to the lodge. I will be there as soon as this matter is finished," Running Otter told his mother.

Yellow Moon nodded and waited for Little Eagle to stop heaving.

Chapter 12

THE DAYS TURNED into weeks and Little Eagle was on the road to healing. She had spent most of her nights in the beginning crying out to God for help getting through this nightmare, but now she found herself giving thanks for the grace and peace that He had given her.

Little Eagle had spent several afternoons in her favorite stop on the moss beneath the trees and she found herself there again today. It was so quiet and peaceful here. She could think, pray, or just relax. She sat leaning against a tree with her eyes closed, listening to the birds that chirped around her. Little Eagle gave a start when she sensed the presence of someone else. When she opened her eyes, Running Otter was standing in front of her with a smile on his face.

"You startled me," she smiled back.

Running Otter sat down on the moss next to Little Eagle. "I have wanted to talk to you for a while now, but I wanted to give you enough time to get past what has happened," he said. "Do you think you are ready for talking?"

Little Eagle nodded that she was.

Running Otter sighed, "I wanted to tell you that if you will come to my side of the fire and be my wife, I will never take another wife. I know you will want some time to think about it, but I would like for us to be a family."

"I will consider what you have said," she responded.

They sat together beneath the trees for a while longer and then Running Otter dismissed himself, leaving Little Eagle alone with her thoughts. She knew there was no going back, even if she had the chance. She would have been considered soiled because she had been the wife of an Indian. As long as God was here with her, it did not matter to her where she was. She would love and serve

God right here. Satan had tried to use Running Otter to wipe her from the face of the earth, but her Heavenly Father intervened. And instead, He turned the situation around and used Running Otter to be her protector and provider. Father Humphrey was right. Running Otter was the most honorable man in the village. Love and hate were choices people make and she chose to love. Her hope was that one day Running Otter might love her.

Later that night, Little Eagle went to Running Otter's side of the fire pit and sat down beside him as he lay on his bed.

"I will be your wife, Running Otter," she said.

Running Otter brushed the side of her face with the back of his fingers. "I have grown very fond of you, Little Eagle. I am pleased that you have come to me," he said softly.

"I have feelings for you, too," she said, placing her hand over his. "You have been an honorable man; always trying to do what you thought was best for me. I am grateful."

Running Otter pulled her down beside him, "I have cared for you for a while now," he told her.

"Really?" she asked with surprise.

"The night we lost our child," he said. "This warrior's heart broke when he heard the Eagle cry and he has loved her ever since," he admitted as he wrapped his arms around her and pulled her close.

About the Author

Vicki lives with her husband Ken on a small farm in Southeast Ohio. She enjoys spending time with her family and caring for the many animals and poultry that call Emerald Hills Farm their home. In addition, she likes flower gardening, crocheting, painting, and of course, writing.